BLUE ROAN COLT

COLT

A NOVEL

also by

DUSTY RICHARDS

Zekial • *The Natural*

The Byrnes Family Ranch Series

Texas Blood Feud • *Between Hell and Texas* • *Ambush Valley*
Blood on the Verde River • *Brothers in Blood* • *A Good Day to Kill*
Arizona Territory • *Pray for the Dead* • *Valley of Bones*
Sharpshooter • *Rage for Vengeance*

The O'Malley Brothers Series

The O'Malleys of Texas • *Dead Aim*

The Brandiron Series

A Bride for Gil • *The Mustanger and the Lady*
The Cherokee Strip • *Gold in the Sun*

The Texas Badge Series

The Texas Badge

The Law Series

Servant of the Law • *Rancher's Law* • *Lawless Land*

BLUE ROAN COLT

A NOVEL

THREE-TIME SPUR AWARD WINNER

DUSTY RICHARDS

with VELDA BROTHERTON

TIREE
PRESS

an imprint of
OGHMA CREATIVE MEDIA

OGHMA

C R E A T I V E   M E D I A

Tiree Press
An imprint of Oghma Creative Media, Inc.
2401 Beth Lane, Bentonville, Arkansas 72712

Library of Congress Cataloging-in-Publication Data

Names: Richards, Dusty, author.
Title: Blue Roan Colt/Dusty Richards.
Description: Second Edition. | Bentonville: Tiree, 2019.
Identifiers: LCCN: 2018961298 | ISBN: 978-1-63373-274-2 (hardcover) | ISBN: 978-1-63373-275-9 (trade paperback) | ISBN: 978-1-63373-276-6 (eBook)
Subjects: BISAC: FICTION/Westerns | FICTION//Historical /World War II | FICTION/Historical
LC record available at: https://lccn.loc.gov/2018961298

Tiree Press trade paperback edition June, 2019

Cover & Interior Design by Casey W. Cowan
Editing by Velda Brotherton and Dennis Doty

This book is a work of historical fiction. Apart from the well-known actual people, events, and locales that figure in the narrative, all names, characters, places, and incidents are the product of the author's imagination or are used fictitiously. Any resemblance to current events or locales, or to living persons, is entirely coincidental.

This one's for Pam

FOREWORD

FOR THIRTY YEARS, DUSTY RICHARDS and I enjoyed a special friendship. We met as struggling writers and found in on another a kindred spirit, both determined to learn our craft. In essence, you might say I was weaned on writing westerns beside the man who would go on to become one of the most successful and prolific writers of the genre. Dusty wrote and published nearly 200 Westerns during his career under his own name and various pseudonyms. He won three Western Writers of America Spur Awards, multiple Will Rogers Medallions, a Western Heritage Award, and many other honors, and one of his later novels—*The Mustanger and the Lady*—was adapted into a full-length motion picture released in 2017. He had the kind of success most writers can only dream about, and I learned more from him than I can possibly describe here.

The most important thing I learned from Dusty, though, was to share my hard-won knowledge freely. Possessed of possibly the world's most generous spirit, he helped countless other struggling writers over the course of his long career, teaching them the ins and outs of chapters and plots, marking up manuscripts, even shoving some of them—like me—into a room with a publisher and barring the door behind. He enjoyed giving others a hand up, and was the rare kind of person that was genuinely happy to see another succeed. I couldn't be more privileged than to have known him and spent so many years helping writers beside him.

To that end, I'm so happy to have been chosen to complete the rewrites and edits for *Blue Roan Colt,* one of Dusty's most touching books. He was working on it himself before the tragic car accident that claimed his life and that of his loving wife, Pat, last year, and his loyal readers will no doubt enjoy this, probably the latest book he had hands on before he was taken from us. I spent several weeks completing what he began, making this book one of his finest, and I'm honored to have been included as having contributed to its completion. *Blue Roan Colt* is about a World War II veteran who pursues his dream of owning a ranch and healing the scars left behind by battle. The story takes the reader through a west only Dusty could portray and tells the heart-wrenching story of the desire, hope, and faith of one man determined to live out his dream despite all obstacles.

Dusty was one of the greatest storytellers I've ever met, and his knowledge of the west and its history was infinite. His books will outlive generations. My profound thanks to Casey Cowan, Oghma Creative Media, and Galway Press for considering me for the continuation of Dusty's great legacy.

—Velda Brotherton
Winslow, Arkansas
January 27, 2019

BLUE ROAN COLT

1

THE WAR DUMPED MARK BACK in New Jersey at Camp Call. All he wanted was to ride a horse to the end of the world and back, but that dream would probably stay just that—a dream, him without a home to go to and all.

The Depression before the damn war caused his grandfather to lose the family's ranch up by Congress where he grew up. He was supposed to inherit the P Bar 9, but now it belonged to some New York broker who wore Gene Autry clothes around the place. He turned it into nothing more than a dude ranch.

Any rodeoing activity would sure be a luxury in his life. Maybe he could manage a ranch for someone. Employment of some sort would have to happen, with his wife Shelia waiting in Phoenix for him. As for that ride cross-country, he'd have to kiss that notion goodbye. Only good thing for sure—he was going home as soon as they got his discharge papers worked up.

It had been four years since he'd marched off to that theater of hell. He never had another chance to be a husband after he climbed on that first bus and went to Fort Leonard Wood in Missouri. After basic, he took a train to New York and went onboard a passenger boat commandeered to carry GI Joes to England.

He hated ships, hated oceans. It was a wonder they didn't get torpedoed going over there. All through that long separation, he missed his wife like other soldiers missed their homes and families. Never, in that span of four plus years, had he ever so much as looked at another woman. Well, maybe looked but that was danged sure all. There were lots of female camp followers in England, plenty of grateful women in France. A mass of widows and Rosie the Riveter kind of gals who sat on stools in New Jersey bars. None were for him. He had a downright pretty wife at home.

After four winters of freezing his ass off in Europe, he was headed back to Phoenix at last, where it barely frosted even in winter.

Surely, he could find a real cattle place that needed him. What with all these soldiers returning to the U.S. of A. there wouldn't be many jobs open for very long. Veterans, they called them. When Congress got done, they were going to get a GI Bill of Rights to go to college and to buy a house. He'd figured a lot of that talk was just bullshit. He simply wanted to be home.

Only partway there, he dropped in to see Sergeant Nelson, the noncom working on his discharge papers.

The red-faced older guy glanced up. "Hey, cowboy. If I coulda got you a bus ticket, I'da sent you home. But they're all booked full."

"Listen, Sarge. If I can get out, I can get my own ass home to Arizona."

"I wondered about that. I can get you fifty bucks cash and your discharge papers tomorrow."

He put his service cap back on. "I'm ready. What time do I need to be here?"

"Two p.m. Two-thirty you'll be free."

Hard to believe he could put the army and that war behind him. He grinned at the noncom. "If you weren't so damn ugly, I'd kiss you."

"No, thanks. You got a wife?"

"Sure. In Phoenix. Shelia's her name. She'll be excited."

"Got any kids?"

He shook his head.

"Well, in a few days, you'll be home and can start working on a family."

"By damn, I'll do that."

The next day, with discharge papers in his hot hands, he left the base about three p.m. and caught a ride across the Hudson River, the driver leaving him in downtown. Busy dang place—noisy too—but he flagged down a cab and, for forty cents, went to the open market trucking district. In the right place at last, he searched for a California trucking firm rig. Inside of an hour, he found an outfit from Bakersfield.

The driver was a balding guy smoking a cigar. Sure enough, he was Italian.

Mark didn't care one way or the other. "Hey, I need to get to Arizona. Are you heading back west?"

"You bet. Can you drive a rig?"

"Been driving army rigs for four years. Drove bob trucks since I was twelve."

"We'll split the driving. I'll buy the eats. What's your name, soldier boy?"

"Mark Shaw."

Vincenzo was the man's first name. He knew that much when they climbed in the cab and headed west to Indiana to pick up a load of pumpkins. Two days later they loaded umpteen hundreds of the orange globes into the trailer and headed for Saint Louis and the Route 66 highway to California.

The new road was only two lanes and went through every town along the way. Vinnie was what he called the old man who knew every place across the country that either served good food or had sharp looking waitresses.

Part of 66 wasn't even paved yet. Construction had been shut off by the war. He found driving Vinnie's old truck as tough on the rutted roadway as an army rig. They had a few flats to change by breaking the casing down and patching the tube. Then they'd hand pump them up again beside the road.

At Flagstaff, where he planned to part with the old man, Vinnie bought him a large chicken-fried steak dinner. They shook hands, ready to say goodbye.

"I'm-ah damn sure sorry to part witcha," the crusty Italian said. "You the best tire pumper I ever hauled. You want to drive a truck cross-country, you call Bakersfield and ask for Tony's Trucking. Dem phone operators all know him. He messes around wid 'em. He'll hire you. I'll tell him all about you."

"Say, you're the straightest shooter I ever met. But I'm going back to Phoenix to find me a ranch manager's job, and the only trucking I plan to do is hauling cattle to market."

Vinnie climbed into his truck. "Yeah, yeah. I'll go watch a Gene Autry film at the movie theater and say there goes my buddy Mark Shaw."

———

DURING THE LAST LEG OF his trip, an old man in a Model A pickup hauled him down through Oak Creek Canyon to Camp Verde. The man's name was Rough Cravens. He owned a ranch east of there. It was a wonder they survived the trip, considering his driving on the hairpin curves with the sorry brakes on the loaded pickup.

The near wrecks never bothered Cravens, but Mark spread his hands on the dash every once in a while to save himself from the next expected crash. In places, the old man fought the steering wheel and raised his hatchet ass off the seat to apply the dull brakes as hard as he could. Down in the canyon, the roadway flattened out and followed a clear creek that reflected the cottonwoods in their golden fall foliage. At last, he could relax. His heart back to normal, he talked with the driver about a ranch job for him.

Cravens knew of a couple of neighbor ranchers who wanted some help. Eager to hear more, Mark took down their names on a small pad with a stub of a pencil. "Any of them have a house for their cowboy? I have a wife in Phoenix who's waiting for me."

"Waiting? How long you been gone?"

"Four long damn years."

"Most women around here done found themselves a new one to rut with."

Mark shook his head. "No, I wrote her regular. She's had hell getting by, but she'll be there waiting for me."

Cravens simply nodded. He heard him, but he never looked convinced of what he'd assured him about Shelia.

All the way down the valley, the aroma of the creosote in his nose was better than Flagstaff's piney smells. Heading home was the most important part of the deal—he'd soon be in Shelia's arms. Whew, that had been a long time for a man to have been without his wife.

"I know about a ranch up in my country. The heirs want to sell it. Cattle ain't been worked since before the war. Mavericks all over the place. It's a mess. But none of us had any help and taking care of what we had was more than we could do."

"What do they call it?"

"Hancock Ranch. It's back up on the Verde and Bloody Basin country. A man could carve a good ranch out of it if he was tough enough."

"What do they want for it?"

"Oh, a couple thousand would suit them, I believe. None of them heirs live around here."

A lot more money than he had in his pocket, for damn sure. But perhaps he could find a moneyman to put up the dough. Would the VA consider a ranch a home? He sure would. Just to be sure he'd remember that name, he scribbled Hancock Ranch down on his pad.

Parting ways with the old man at the base of the mountain, he shook his hand and thanked him. After telling him he'd see him again sometime, he stepped out into the bright afternoon. The Arizona warmth was one of the things he missed the most in Europe. The sun came out over there, but even in summer time, his bones stayed cold. He had real sun shining on him while he ran to catch up with an older De Soto. The driver offered him a ride to Phoenix. He said his name was Dillon and shook hands like a dead fish.

Mark tossed his war bag in the trunk before he got in. Several canvas water bags hung all over the car and gallon jugs of water sat behind the front seat. Obviously, Dillon was ready for the narrow road that climbed to the top of the mountain.

The engine roared and the man let out the clutch. They were mountaintop bound. He kept looking at his heat gauge. Gravel crunched under the tires on the narrow roadway and the stench of the engine filled the air.

"How are we doing?"

"Oh, she ain't in the red yet, but she's getting close. Don't worry. I've got plenty of water. Last time she boiled over going up this mountain."

"Should we stop and cool her off?"

"Ain't no place to do that here."

That was a pure fact. The gurgling of the radiator soon told them they were about as far as they could go.

After nudging the car against the bluff side, Dillon braked and shut off the key. "You get out, get rocks, and block all the wheels. I'll hold my foot hard on the brake. We'll have to let her cool awhile."

Mark agreed and squeezed out his side. Rocks lay everywhere. Finding the size he wanted, he soon had the tires well blocked. Dillon huffed like he'd done all the work and complained about getting a cramp in his leg holding the pedal down.

"You're fine now."

How in the world would the next car coming up the hill ever pass them on the narrow ledge?

Soon, he and Dillon found themselves coaxing the driver of an older Ford coupe past the disabled De Soto. He would have sworn that half of the man's outside tire treads hung out over the cliff, but he kept at it, screwing his bearded face up one or two times when he skidded close to the edge. Mark sucked in his breath, scared he'd have to stand there helpless and watch the old Ford tumble right down to the bottom, taking the fella with it. But he made it, good and safe. After thanking them, he waved and drove on.

Dillon kept laying his hand real fast on the hood, shaking his head and muttering, "We're fine. We have plenty of water."

The car finally cooled. After refilling the radiator, the old man pulled out for the crest. She boiled over again about fifty feet from the top, but another half-hour of sitting in the road ditch and she had cooled down. They headed, at long last, for Prescott. All the locals called it Preskit. It was near evening when Dillon steered the car into the city and stopped so they could eat supper in the famous Palace Bar on Whiskey Row. After the great meal, he headed down the mountain with the sun setting, over towards Wickenburg.

In places, Mark worried the De Soto's grinding brakes might send them off the steep curvy mountain road, but before midnight the old car carried them into Phoenix. Dillon drove to the former tourist court on east Van Buren where Shelia had rented them a place. She wrote him that the court owner had changed the cabins into small apartments. The tourist business had been slow in Phoenix because of gas rationing. No one could travel much during the war.

He got out and thanked Dillon. Nervous and excited, he slung the war bag onto his shoulder, looking at the open door of the first run-down cabin. A woman stood smoking a cigarette with a hand on her hip.

"You looking for company, soldier boy?"

"No. I'm looking for my wife, Shelia. She lives in number five."

"If she ain't home, come back and see me."

Her proposition disgusted him. He was proud of himself—a married man. He didn't need to be looking at other women. Not with his wife waiting for him only fifty feet away. The lights were out in number five. He knocked on the door, his heart beating like a runaway horse. He was downright ready to embrace his lovely wife.

"Who's there?" a sleepy voice shouted.

"It's your husband, darling."

Inside, hollering and shouting erupted. Hearing enough, he kicked in the cheese-box door with one heavy combat boot. It busted wide open. A woman screamed from under a blanket on the bed. A man pulling on pants danced across the floor and rushed out the door like Mark might be gonna shoot him. He damn-sure would've if he'd 'a had him a gun. As it was, he ran after the man, who high-tailed it across the parking lot and behind another cabin.

Furious and looking for someone to blame, Mark turned back to stare at the woman, who was pulling on a skirt and sweater. This wasn't the Shelia he married. This wasn't the teenager he had held with so much respect in the six months they were married before he went off to war. This was some cheating woman he didn't recognize. No matter how hard he wished it, she was Sheila all right. Sour vomit rose from behind his tongue.

He barely heard her pleading—how hard she'd had it, how she'd tried and tried to even find enough food to eat, how it was all his fault because he left her. He didn't hear half her words. An evil enemy cornered him in that room, making him dizzy and sick to his stomach.

She came over to hug him and plead for his forgiveness. Her and her mussed hair and smeared lipstick. Wanting none of that, he shoved her back on the bed and staggered to the doorway and out to Van Buren street. He flagged down a ride that took him over to Mesa. His old man lived with a Mexican wife somewhere in that vicinity.

After several dead-end tries, he met a man on the street who told him that his dad lived down at Chandler on a cotton farm. He hitched a ride with a husband and wife to the road where they lived and walked the mile down to an adobe *jacal* in the middle of the tall, ripe cotton. No lawn, just dirt and oil spots with tractors and farm machinery parked all around the place.

There were some black-eyed kids who ran to tell the people in the house a real soldier was out there. His dad came to the doorway and blinked at the sight of him.

Dad's hair and mustache had turned snow white. He looked twenty years older than when Mark saw him last.

"That you, Mark?"

"It ain't Saint Nick." They embraced. He got kind of teary and so did Dad. When it was over, both men snuffed and wiped their eyes.

Dad slapped him on the back. "I didn't expect you to come by so soon. How's your wife?"

"I don't have one anymore." He just wished everyone would stop talking about his wife.

"Gawd, I'm sorry. I should've taken her in, but me and Lenore have three kids now. They're your half-brothers. Except Lillie, she's your half-sister. Times have been hard. I was doing day labor. We lived in an abandoned adobe. Nothing...." He looked down at callused hands like he was ashamed.

Not sure what to say, Mark cleared his throat. "I know you must have tried. Do you still have a saddle?"

"Sure, why?" The faded blue eyes glanced up.

"I want to borrow it. I'm going to get me a horse and ride it to hell and back. Maybe find myself again somewhere out there." He gave a toss of his head to anywhere.

"You have a horse?"

"No, but I can get one. I need to borrow the saddle."

"Aw, son, you sure that's what you want to do? Get a job before they're all gone. There's so many soldiers coming home. Get a car and save your money. They say this next depression will be ten times worse than the last one."

"I don't care. I'm going to try to drive the madness in my mind away."

"It must have been hell."

"Sure was, but the worst is coming home and finding a wife cheating on me. Things are so different from what I wanted them to be. I can't tell you, but I am about to explode. I need to get away—clear my head."

Dad didn't seem all that concerned. Instead, he turned to point to the woman. "You know my wife, Lenore?"

Mark shook his head to clear it and studied the short, dark woman in her bright red and blue Mexican dress, her belly showing the baby inside. The snow on the mountaintop had not hurt his old man one bit.

"Good to see you again." Right away he could see what Dad saw in her. She had nice eyes.

When she looked up, she smiled real sweet at him. "I heard you say you want to ride away on a horse?" She made a face.

"Yes, I want to ride to the end of the world. Leave it all behind."

The caring in her dark eyes was believable. "I know a witch lives over in Gilbert that can help. She has treated many soldiers and they got better."

"Thanks. The horse ride's all I need."

"Well." She shrugged. "Have you eaten lately?"

"I'm fine."

"Come, I have some enchiladas left. I will feed you. You look thin."

He ate her fare and then his dad showed him the saddle—a high back cantle western saddle, it had a good high fork to dally rope on. He'd kept it soaped and ready for use.

"I can't pay you for it now, but how much will I owe you?"

"Is forty dollars fair?"

"Yep. I'll pay you whenever I get back."

They shook hands. That evening, he slept in a hammock under a squaw shade of palm fronds behind the house. It sure beat a foxhole with mortars flying over. In the night, he awoke to hear his father and Lenore talking about him in Spanish. Then they made love across the shelter in their hammock. His heart ached for what he'd lost—and him not doing anything to cause it but fighting that blamed war.

Laying there in the quiet dark, looking up at a sky full of stars, he vowed that tomorrow he would go look for a horse. All he wanted now was to get away and not look back. He knew an Indian who lived up by Lehi who caught wild horses. His name was "Dirty Shirt" Jones. He could find him a suitable mustang to ride. A famous remount stallion had gotten loose and ran free for several years with those wild horses and had sired some damn good colts. He needed one of those outcroppings for himself.

In the morning, along with his newfound half-kinfolk, he ate flour tortillas wrapped around scrambled eggs and pork chorizo with plenty of hot salsa on them. They were sweet kids and excited that their *gringo* brother was a real soldier. He thought back to his mother, who probably would frown at his father remarrying and producing so many little Mexican kids. But she had died years before, so that was that.

His mother's family had owned the ranch that he'd hoped to inherit as a boy. They buried her in Phoenix when he was in his mid-teens. She was a straight-backed woman who could, according to his father, stretch dollars until George Washington screamed. Then she made the Indian on the buffalo nickel cry real tears when she shoved him in a moldy old piggy bank. What would she have said about his planned horse ride? No telling, but she'd 've had something to say to him before he left, had she been alive. He still recalled her on that day he left for the army. Standing out in the yard, the wind whipping her hair. She raised one hand and held it there till he couldn't see her any longer. Thinking about her, like to made him cry.

The next morning he left the saddle at his father's place, promising to come back for it. He went out to the highway and, before he walked back to Chandler, caught a ride on to Mesa. He'd stashed his war bag in a locker at the National Guard office the day before and they said it would be all right until he needed it again. Looking for a ride to Lehi from Mesa when he got out of the nice man's '37 Pontiac, he walked downtown to the Indian Pony Parking Lot. There was an entire city block for Indians to leave their teams, single horses, and wagons while they shopped.

He was sort of hanging around, looking things over, when he noticed a young squaw on one of the wagons. It was Alma Cornbird, a girl he'd known during high school. She smiled and spoke to him in Spanish. Wrapped in a bright colored blanket, she was less than five feet tall. Hard to tell her shape from that, but she wasn't fat or pregnant like his stepmother. She was a full blood Pima or Maricopa, or maybe she came from a related tribe that lived around there.

"Aren't you Carl Shaw's son?" she asked when she quit talking in Spanish. Everyone knew his father.

"Yes, my name is Mark."

"You are a soldier. Is the war really over?" she asked in English, like she could not believe it.

"*Sí.* I'm still dressed like a soldier because I just got back from there. They can never cause another war. We bombed them flat."

"Do you have a wife?"

There it was about a wife again. He shook his head. "Not anymore."

"Me, either. I mean, I have no husband. He was killed in the Pacific last year."

"Was he an Indian?"

"No, his name was Jeff Downs."

"I knew him. I'm sorry. I played football for Mesa High with him all four years."

"It was such a shame. Where are you going now?"

"To see Dirty Shirt Jones. I need a horse."

She nodded, then sat down cross-legged in the little shade from her buckboard. "If you buy some wieners, we can cook them here and sleep under my wagon tonight. Tomorrow, we can eat the rest for breakfast and I will take you up there to his place. It is way too late to go home tonight." She shrugged. "Without lights, we might get run over on the highway."

"Sure, I can do that, buy some wieners and buns. How will we cook them?"

"There is plenty of wood around here. I will have the fire going when you get back."

He went to the nearest small family grocery store and bought a package of a dozen wieners, some buns, and Oreo cookies, plus some Milky Way candy bars. Good to see them again on the store shelf.

Yes, Alma. The war is over. They even have candy bars coming back.

Alma had a good cooking fire blazing when he returned. She sat on an old rug for their place to eat. When he drew the Milky Way out of the bag and showed her, her eyes went wide.

"You bought that for me?"

"Sure."

She stood on her toes and pursed her mouth to kiss him. He bent over and liked doing it. Then she hooked his neck to keep him down there and kissed his cheek twice more. "You are a *mucho* sweet *hombre.*"

What would she have had to eat without his franks and buns? He didn't bother to ask.

She cooked two at a time on long sticks. Then, when they were kinda burned black in places, she took them off by squeezing a bun around them, lathered them in mustard, and handed them both to him.

"You eat one," he said.

"No, I cook more."

"That fire will last. Eat with me."

She closed one eye to stare at him. "You want to spoil a squaw?"

Did he want to spoil her? Why not? He'd fought a war that cost him his wife, didn't he deserve some rewards? He smiled and nodded. "Yes, and more."

"Oh." She raised her eyebrows. "More than that? I better eat with you then."

They both laughed, and he halfway rose and kissed her again. The sun was fast fading and the fire reflected off her dark face. A nice-looking, little woman still wrapped in her blanket, though it was not cold. He knew her plans for the two of them for the night but was in no rush.

They ate two apiece and left the rest for in the morning. She put them and the buns inside the hinged wooden box on her buckboard, so some stray dog wouldn't find them. Then she brought out a painter's stained canvas for a ground cloth and made them a bed under her wagon.

The fire was about burned down, but she had more fuel stacked up for the morning. The parking lot was nearly empty. Only two other families were spending the night there. They were across the grassless city block from them. Streetlights kept things in sight. Her two buckskin horses were through munching on the Johnson grass hay. She probably cut that forage for them off a bar ditch bank on the way to town.

Squatting down before him, she began to unlace his boots. The grin on her face made him know she was pleased he planned to stay the night with her.

"We can undress under the covers," she whispered.

He agreed. He didn't even feel bad for what he was set on doing. Somehow, it seemed right that this pretty girl would meet his needs in such a peaceful place.

Up before dawn, she chewed on her third Oreo cookie of the day and had the fire going to cook a wiener breakfast while he dressed. He sat on his butt and re-laced his boots, knowing why his father had married Lenore. Mexican and Indian women were sure different from fussy gringos when making love. They were fierce at it—no barriers, no fussing, simply driving for the end.

She took him to see Dirty Shirt Jones. The tall, broad-shouldered bachelor was older than Mark, a full-blood who got his name from wearing the same shirt until he wore it out. The horse-catcher stared at the squaw sitting out on her wagon seat.

He nodded at Mark. "It is a shame her man died."

"Lots of good men died." Blinking back tears, he stared across the valley, seeing some of his best buddies standing all in a row. He reached out, but they were gone now. He shook his head to clear the memories. "I need a good horse."

"I know where there is a sorrel stallion, maybe three, maybe four. I have tried to catch him many times. He is pretty as his sire, the famous stallion. If you help and we catch two or three more, you can have him. We only catch him, he costs forty dollars."

He thought about that for a moment. "I'll go get my saddle and be back in two days. We'll go get him and those others."

Dirty Shirt motioned toward the woman with his head, his braids dangling. "Is she coming along to cook?"

Mark studied her sitting out there in the yard on the spring seat just watching him. "I'll ask her."

"We will need some *frijoles.*"

"I can get some supplies. Two days and I will return."

Dirty Shirt bobbed his head in agreement.

Outside Jones's *jacal,* he stopped to speak to Alma. "I need to go back to Mesa, then go to my father's and get my saddle. I'll meet you back at Mesa. Then we'll go horse chasing, if you'd like to go along."

"Me go, too?" She pointed at her chest in disbelief.

"If you want to."

A small smile crossed her copper lips and she wrinkled her narrow, once-broken nose at him. "I have a saddle closer than his place that you can use. Save you a long trip."

"Good, then we can get some supplies tomorrow and I'll use your saddle."

She stopped and lowered her head. "You can use it, but it is not really mine."

"Who owns it?" Before the words were out of his mouth, he realized it must have been Jeff's.

He touched her hand and whispered, "I am so sorry."

"I will be fine. I will be fine, but thanks for being so caring."

After the trip to the Lehi store to buy a hundred-pound sack of *frijoles,* flour, and lard, she bought some dried figs, dried apples, and raisins from some of her Indian friends. He bought a cheap straw western hat to keep his head out of the sun. The two of them gathered the saddle and some cooking utensils. They needed a few things from her small frame house, including an old sidewall tent. That night, they slept in her bed and didn't leave to go to Dirty Shirt's until the sun rose to wake them.

On the way, they washed in the wide irrigation canal. No one came by while they were naked in the water. Wading in water up to her chin, she covered her mouth and started giggling.

"One day, some of us were bathing right here. A white man came driving by and kept watching us and looking back until he drove his truck off in the canal. We all laughed. We dried off and left him there. I guess he got a wrecker 'cause his truck was underwater except for the top of the cab. Next time we came here it was gone. Served him right for looking at naked Indian women." She laughed some more. It felt good to join her.

They arrived at Dirty Shirt's place at dusk. She built a fire a short ways from the house and made Indian fry bread. He showed up in time to help them eat it.

Sitting cross-legged on the ground, he said, "I am glad you are bringing her along. She can damn sure cook."

She looked sideways at him and frowned. "Why don't you have a woman of your own?"

"I would have to catch more horses to feed her."

"That would not hurt a big man like you."

"Why should I have one? I can go to the dance and find plenty drunk ones to make love to me."

"You are worthless," she said in Spanish.

"You find me a pretty one. I will think about making her my wife."

"Hear what he wants me to do?" She pointed at Dirty Shirt.

"Find him one." Mark chuckled, and she made a face at him too.

"You are no better than him."

Everyone laughed, and Mark felt really good for the first time since he couldn't remember when.

2

ON THE NEXT DAY, THEY worked their way toward the Fort Mc-Dowell Reservation, Alma driving the wagon. Tied on behind were four extra horses to relay-chase the wild ones.

This country, dry as it was, looked so good. Mark had missed mountains in the distance, the smell of sage in bloom, cactus reaching into a blue sky. The canal was a surprise to most, not expecting to see water in any quantity in Arizona. Just showed how little folks knew. Granite Reef Dam was the last diversion dam on the Salt River Project above Phoenix. There, they crossed the last bridge over the canal and turned east to parallel the river.

"Let's pull over here and make camp." He pointed toward his choice.

Tough as she was, Alma looked relieved, though she never would admit to being tired. She reined the team into a flat spot above the river. Dry as this country was, flash floods could sweep into all the low places if a rainstorm hit upriver. He took a quick look around and nodded at the choice for camping the night. She tied the reins and hopped down.

Dirty Shirt stayed mounted. "I will look for signs of the band before dark." He rode off to scout the countryside without waiting for a reply.

The Indian never seemed to grow weary. Mark climbed down to help Alma make camp. To the west, a fingernail moon hung in the silver sky. Along the horizon, mountains cut purple jags.

"It'll be dark soon. Let's get this canvas unloaded." He jumped up in the wagon and tossed out the poles and ropes while she slid one roll of canvas painter's cloth past the tailgate.

She went to unload the wall tent. "Will we need this?"

"Let's not use it here. Just the cloths for shelter should be enough. It's a clear, dark night to look at the stars." He liked being out in the open with land as far as the eye could see.

She had a shade made from a canvas painter's cloth and poles with iron pins on the ends to support it. He drove stakes into the ground and tied off some ropes to hold it up.

"Where in thunder did you get all those canvas sheets?" They even had grommets in them for the pins and to tie the ropes too.

She shrugged. "Jeff come home with them one time. Did not say where they came from. He was always gathering things up he thought we might use. I had to get rid of a lot of it. Just junk to me. Guess he saw some good in them. But these I see good in."

When she talked about her man, even mentioned his name, she got all upset. So, he tried not to bring him up. Mark was fine for her company, but the loss of her husband still strickened her. Jeff's saddle was a good one and she'd kept it. She took it careful-like to a spot near camp and worked soap into the leather while Mark gathered wood for the fire.

By the time Dirty Shirt returned with no news of signs of the band, a fire crackled out front of the shelter and a pot of beans left from the night before bubbled at its edge next to a gurgling coffee pot.

Mark fast took to having her for a wife. Though to him, they weren't married. To her, all it took was a small Indian ceremony to make it legal. That was okay with him. Men needed a woman around to keep things on track. She could ably set up camp while they searched for the young horses. The meals were frijoles and fried bacon twice a day. They usually skipped lunch in their searching because they made such wide circles.

One day while staring in all directions, again in vain with no sign of wild horses, Mark hollered at Dirty Shirt. "For all we've found, you must've seen all those horses in a *peyote* dream. Or was you just drunk on cheap whiskey or homemade watermelon wine?"

"You will not think that when you see them. Just over that next rise. You are nothing but a crazy white man. What do you know?" The Indian laughed and spurred his horse to run in circles while he whooped.

"Oh, that's a good idea, you crazy Indian. Scare them all away."

The following day, Dirty Shirt rode back to Alma's wagon where Mark had returned to get a drink. This time, he wasn't hollering.

He pointed. "Just over there, beyond that rise. Several mares and colts, and a stallion that led bands."

"Not sure we can use them. We need a bachelor party of young horses."

Dirty Shirt shook his head. "I do know this. Just thought I could prove I have not been drunk or having visions from *peyote*. We will keep going and we will find what we are looking for." The two men had been swapping the five horses to ride so as not to wear out any. She fed the ponies Johnson grass hay that she hand-cut each day, so they were stout enough only using them every other day to make their long trips.

Late one afternoon, after he had checked the setting sun, he turned around to the east and spotted a red horse leading some others off the far slopes. They were headed for the cottonwoods along the Verde, coming in the red sunlight. The stallion's shiny hide looked deeper than blood in the bright reflection above the golden cottonwoods. The trees had only started to turn yellow down there, because it was warmer in the valley than up by Flagstaff.

"There is the red one." He pointed them out.

The nod of the Indian's head was all he saw. Then he left, spurring his horse. Mark followed, splashing across the Verde, knee-deep on his mount, then up the sandy bank.

"I said they were here." Dirty Shirt shouted at him, lashing his horse with the reins.

"Damn, he's sure pretty." Spurring the bay horse, he kept up. Saddle leather creaked, and horses grunted.

Wind in his face and headed for a goal at last, he forgot about memories of watery muck trenches along with the rattle of machinegun fire filling the air. He flew with bald eagles, his mount jumping over downed brush and scrambling for his footing in loose gravel, cat-hopping to reach the next bench above them. The flashing hooves of their mounts made rocks and gravel and clods of grass fly. The evergreen sap smell of junipers in his nose, he went right when Jones veered left around some larger ones. Riding flat out, they climbed Four Peaks Mountain from the base toward the sharp points on top.

In two hours of this pressed pursuit, the hard-breathing saddle horses were covered in foamy lather. Jones drew up and Mark followed. In the fading light of day, the loose ones had somehow lost them. But that never mattered. He had already caught the fever of the hunt. Many times, when he caught sight of the animals in the span of the chase, his heart pounded hard in his chest. The red horse looked like a large ruby in a golden ring gleaming in the sun going down over the far mountainside.

Gone again.

But they would catch him. One day soon.

No matter what it cost him, he had to have that sorrel for his own. That horse was going to free him of exploding grenades and incoming artillery rounds killing his buddies only a few yards away. Why had he lived through that when his buddies hadn't? Maybe his slain comrades were in a better place. He wished he would quit catching glimpses of them all bloody and battered. Following after him. Never speaking, just watching. He had no idea where they had gone on to, but there must be a master plan.

Late that night, under a sky filled with stars, snug in his and her bedroll, Alma whispered in his ear. "Thank you for bringing me and being so good to me. I will try to be worth it."

Embarrassed, he finally answered her. "You are worth it, just for that good cooking." *And being good company for me,* but he didn't say that aloud for fear of embarrassing her.

The next few days were not so satisfying—always chasing but never catching the bachelor herd. Once more seeing them disappear in the distance. They had to do more to catch the wild horses.

"We have to build two traps and drive the horses into one or the other enclosures," Jones said.

Mark agreed. With only a hand-ax and small bow, the two set to work. It proved to be hard to assemble fencing from dead trees and tie them together with baling wire to make a corral, but the two catch pens were finally done. If the free horses went right or left at the spooks made from hanging Alma's long, wild, paint-covered canvas sheets across their route, those wild ones would be caught.

Five days of hard riding and falling into their bedrolls with weary bones, and things finally went right for the kickoff of their drive. The bachelors showed up for a drink of water from the river like the last time. Alma was mounted on one of Jones's horses as well. She needed no saddle. She rode a horse like a tick anyway. On horseback, each rider moved in slow from three sides to where the wild ones drank knee-deep in the swirling, murky Verde.

Red took a quick drink, then sniffed the air with caution, throwing drops of water in rainbow colors before lowering his head to take another. Even at a distance, the stallion had a wild glint in his dark eyes. Lots of white around them. Seemed a shame to throw a rope on such a wild and free animal. But he had to have him. He'd sure be a real bastard to break. Mark knew his kind well, but the fast approaching challenge of owning such a fine horse swelled in his chest till his heart thudded in his throat. It was all he could think about.

He'd heard no enemy or even friendly artillery in the days since they started this chase. No more waking up ready to pick up his weapon when the fight urges came over him. He slept, without all the Battle of the Bulge desperation of earlier nights when he was first back on U.S. soil. Alma had laid, sleeping peacefully beside him, quieting his demons, chasing that other life back into the shadows.

This horse-gathering business had driven away the gawdamn war's picture. It was clear out of his mind when Jones shouted, "Let's go!" on that crisp early morning.

The three of them tore off to chase the horses into one of their well-planned traps. Half rearing in shock, the red one slung his body around in a great spray of water and lunged for the sandy bank. The frantic animal lost his footing for a moment and went down in the water, but his head never went under. In a flash of wet horsehide, he leaped for the bank in the wild way that Mark expected from him. His shrill screams mobilized the others against the serious trouble at hand.

The race was on. Mark checked on Alma coming from his left side to ford the river he was halfway across. They formed a line, with Jones in the lead. His unblocked black hat set hard on his head and the eagle feather attached to it whipped his brim. Mark rode fast after them. Slanting his head, he caught sight of Alma on the brown gelding hot on his pony's heels.

The whole secret of a trap was to fool them into entering it, get them inside, then slap the gate shut. When the wild ones spooked, not expecting the crazy paint-stained canvas to be strung up in their way, they never hesitated and went left. Headed, at full speed, right for that enclosure.

Jones jumped off his horse and ran faster than Shaw ever would have believed he could. Dust puffed from under his boots, his arms whirl-winding in a race to pull the wire gate shut. He slumped down before it, out of breath.

Alma pointed, clapping her hands. "I really like to see Jones run." Joyous laughter broke through her words. "He wouldn't run that hard to catch a good-looking woman."

It was true. The dash Jones made would have beaten any track team's efforts. In that moment of pure excitement, Mark could have whipped the entire German army singlehanded. The six young horses were captured and in the pen.

Whew!

The next morning, Alma woke him to say breakfast was ready. She did not look as if she liked such wild horse captures. Though the worse for wear, she looked so pretty with her hair down and the colorful dress of blues, reds, and greens. He wanted to sweep her into his arms, but he didn't. It was not yet time to do so. Let her be the first to make such a declaration.

She went to the fire to fix him a plate, her bare toes showing when the long dress swished. How had he found such a beautiful woman who cared so much for him? He was no longer alone, and it felt so good to have her. He stood on top of the bedroll and pulled on his pants. Too many stickers and burrs for him on the gravely ground to expose his own bare soles.

"Are you sorry about all the hard work?" He sat to pull on his boots.

"No. I am as proud as you are to have them caught, but—" She winced at her own movements to walk. "Perhaps we should wait a while before we have another such roundup."

He wrapped her up in his arms and she threw back her head to laugh. His mouth smothered her with kisses. He couldn't help hisself, she was so danged pretty. Afraid how she might act, he held his breath, and then let it out when her powerful small arms clutched him, her strength unbelievable. She'd used it for everything they did. He now had the big Red and this small, sweet Indian woman. How did a man like him dare be so happy?

"What will you do now?" she asked.

"We need to break them and have us some stout ranch horses to gather wild cattle on and build us a ranch."

"I thought you were going to try to get the war out of you?" She frowned.

"I plan to do that too. We're going to look over a ranch we may own some day on what I call our vacation or leave, whatever you call it."

"You say us, over and over. Does that mean I can go, too?"

Shocked that she should wonder such a thing, he studied her hard. "You're already part of this deal. A big part."

She screamed with joy and tackled him.

There were some hot springs up on the Verde. Maybe a day or two in them might loosen her sore back and muscles. Though he hated to admit it, his, too, needed a good hot soaking. It would be good for the both of them. His Injun woman. They both needed someone, and they should be able to solve lots of challenges in the future by working them out together.

He released her. "We have to halter break the new ponies to lead. Then there are full grown horses that have probably only been handled as yearlings that need to be gelded." He pointed out one of them—a big, strong bay. "That one is still a stallion. See the scars from him challenging stallions with bands of mares? They can be handled, but they're all powerful, head-slinging, fear-filled critters to tame. You bet."

Roped, the ponies fought for their lives. Mark wished for boot heels instead of his combat boots—skiing around on the gravelly ground and holding on to the lariat to snub each horse was no fun. He had a bay on the line, number three to tie up. A star in his forehead gave him his name.

He gave a good battle, hoofs kicking high in the sky, head tossing and mane flying. His screams sounded near human. But men won out over animals. Star was finally snubbed and fitted with a halter. Mark slipped a rope around his flank, threaded it between his front legs and through his halter ring. Despite kicking and snorting, he was soon tied close to a nearby stout juniper tree. In one last effort to get away, Star jerked his head high. The rope around his flank closed on his back and soon put an end to his head-slinging and fighting himself.

For a moment, Mark rubbed the sweaty neck, spoke soft words to the animal. Soft brown eyes settled and gazed at him. "Don't worry, it will be good, the place we'll take you to." He felt sorry for an instant that this wild and beautiful animal could no longer run free. Then he patted him. "You will be a good friend."

They took the exhausted animals one at a time to the river between two of their saddle horses to water. The morning was a wild rodeo arena-like event with flashing teeth and attempts to kick both handlers. So far, he and Jones had avoided those full hoof impacts. No surprise it took several hard-working hours just to start their training.

But the pen was not a good place to work horses. It was sloping and tough ground to work on foot. They needed to take the captives back to Jones's place to be better handled. But two riders and one wild horse would be a slow way to move all of them there over thirty miles one way.

"I can go get some Indian boys with horses to help you take them back." Alma kept busy, dishing out bowls of *frijoles* from the pot on the fire.

Hot and sweaty from the day's work, both men were seated on the ground in their camp.

Mark turned to Jones. "What do you think?"

He nodded. "I think we should do that."

Mark turned to her. "I guess we better do that."

Everyone grinned. It was a relief to have the hardest part with these horses done with.

"I'll ride one of the saddle horses. I may not be back until tomorrow or the next day. Can you men find yourself food?" She looked up from under the well-worn straw cowboy hat for their reply.

"We can. Not well, but we can. Do we need you to get some things for us to eat?" Though Mark assured her, Jones kept quiet. Women were supposed to cook for their men, in his mind.

She nodded. "But if we are going back to Lehi, it can wait."

Jones nodded hard. "We got too damn many horses at one time."

"Naw. We'll need them to round up those mavericks."

"I don't know about that."

"Hey, we've got the horse flesh to do it."

"That may be too damn much work, too."

"Aw, come on." Worried about losing Jones, he scooted closer to him. "You aren't going to give up on me."

"Maybe, maybe not."

"Maybe?" He hated to think of doing this without Dirty Shirt.

Jones's nod looked encouraging, but he had no way to tell what the man was really thinking. Before then, Jones'd sounded real interested in the business of finding a way to get ahold of that abandoned ranch. But their job of snubbing these horses had become a tough chore and might have been more than the Indian wanted any part of.

Busy eating his beans, Mark told Alma to be careful on her trip.

She sat beside him, spread out her skirt, and agreed she would before she began to eat. "I can stay and help you two this afternoon, if you want."

"No, getting us some help to move them would be better than if you stayed."

"That would break them good. Dragging them that far." Jones chuckled.

"It would be interesting." Mark's lunch complete, he rose, bent over, and kissed her. At last it was the right and proper thing to do.

She smiled at him. "I will do my best to bring you back some men."

"I'd saddle you a horse, but we need both of them."

She wrinkled her nose. "That is okay. I can go bareback."

He looked at Jones. "Well, shall we try to water some more of them?"

Jones nodded, straining to get on his knees, then rose. "Oh, big job."

Mark laughed and headed for the corral, still a bit worried Jones would quit on him. He needed him bad. Dragging the captives one at a time between their two saddled mounts was no easier with one than any of the others. Every one of the horses put up a battle, like they were trying to make sure the men knew who was boss. That would not last.

The sorrel balked the minute they started him down the steep mountainside. Kicking and struggling to get away from his handlers, the horse fell on his side twice just getting to the bottom and the river. All that dumb jughead wanted was loose from his handlers. Not even the idea of a drink tamed him down. By the time he sucked up his fill and they headed him back to the pen, he was behaving a little better. One after the other, he and Jones dragged each pony to water. One thing they didn't have to do was make them drink. The blamed animals were more thirsty and wore out than the two of them.

Finally, the last one was urged back from the river, hitched to a juniper tree for the night, and fed some of Alma's hand cut hay.

Leading the weary mounts into the pen, Mark followed Jones, closed the gate, stretched, and yawned big. "I sure hope she can find us some riders."

Jones nodded. "She could convince you it is raining. I think she is a *bruja.*" Then he laughed and clapped Mark on the shoulder. "Too damn much work."

Mark didn't like the sound of that. Both remarks gave him the shivers. That Jones might quit was only a bit less worrying than him calling Alma a witch. He had never considered that being possible. Lost maybe over the death of her mate, but not a mystic or anything like one. He'd found her a real bed-full of a woman for such a small body and a damn hard worker, but she was not a *bruja.*

When they finished the rest of the chores, they settled beside the campfire and ate more beans. Bone-tired, they crawled into their bedrolls. A loud noise woke Mark in the middle of the night, and Jones bolted upright when he did. Someone was coming.

"Who is that?" Jones asked, peering into the darkness.

"It's a big truck."

In the headlights, a shadow climbed out of the truck cab.

"It's Alma. Where did she get a stock truck?" And how would he ever pay for it? No telling.

"Mark," she called out. "Do you remember Noah Gaines?" She led a big man wearing coveralls with his name on them to him.

"Sure, we played football." He stuck his hand out to shake the guy's hand.

"I remembered that, too," Gaines said. "She said you have some horses you need hauled over to Lehi."

"We sure do." He turned to Alma. "How did you find him?"

"He was delivering and busy unloading feed at the Lehi Store when I rode up. We talked, and he said he owed you a favor."

"Hey, you don't owe me this much. We'll sure pay you for this business. May take us some time, but you haul our horses, you'll be paid."

Gaines looked around in the glow cast by the truck's headlights. "Don't worry none about that. Where can I back up so it'll be easy to get those broncs in the truck?"

"Over there." Jones led Gaines to a sharp lip.

He studied the ground and agreed, then went for his truck and backed in place. The vehicle set, Mark and Jones went to saddle two horses.

"I hope we survive doing this in the dark." Jones pulled his cinch tight and threaded it in by the starlight.

"We have to."

"Maybe we will, but we will damn sure earn it."

"Nothing is free in this world."

"Damn sure that's right." The wild horses proved stubborn. Looked like they'd gained back the energy spent earlier, too. They fought, they balked, they screamed, they sweated, they kicked—but finally, they were loaded.

"You need to go along with him," Mark told Jones. "He will need you to help to unload those wild mustangs. Take two saddle horses as well and I'll be down later."

Jones nodded and led the well-behaved horses into the truck, too. He looked relieved to be going along. Hopefully that didn't mean he was going to walk away once there. It would be hard to lose the hard-working Indian who had also become a friend. Mark wanted to say something to him to convince him the worst was behind them, but he knew better and so would Jones. It was not easy working with wild animals or building a ranch. Lord, he hoped the man stayed with him.

"We'll be back at your place by dark tomorrow," Mark said, closing the passenger side door.

"I will be asleep," Jones said.

Mark stepped back and shouted thanks to Gaines. Then he stood back as Alma slipped under his arm and he affectionately hugged her to his side.

"You did great. Gaines never said how much I owed him for this?"

She shook her head. "I didn't ask him."

He bent over and kissed her. They shed their clothes on the way to their bedroll. In minutes, they were in each other's arms.

Later in the night, he got up under the stars to empty his bladder. A couple of coyotes yapped as he stood to savor the night in the cool, soft wind. How good it was to be free of those bombs bursting inside his skull. At last, he went back to the bed, easy so he wouldn't waken her. She needed her rest, too. All the while they fought the animals, she'd been right in there, lending a hand where she could, and cooking for them, as well. What a lucky man he was to have found such a woman after his bad experiences with Sheila. She would be a perfect helpmate in his battle to build a ranch and a new life. The best part about that was he loved her, and she seemed to love him, too. He could not imagine that she would ever betray him either. Content, he stared at the scattering of stars for a long while and fell asleep listening to her soft breathing.

3

THE LONG, HOT, DUSTY DRIVE from Fort McDowell to Mesa seemed as endless as the day. Mark perched on the spring seat, keeping up a long conversation with Alma about the Hancock Ranch and his plans to buy it.

"I tell you, if there's any way in the world for me to get that ranch, I'm going to do it. All I got in my pocket is a bit under three hundred dollars and no job. So, it won't be easy."

Alma just kept listening and driving her team. When they pulled into Jones's yard, he was still scheming. He could think of nothing else ever since Rough Craven told him about the abandoned ranch stocked with mavericks. He wanted that place worse than anything.

She wrapped the reins and stared at him for a moment, dark eyes flashing.

"What?" She sure looked like she had something to say.

"I think you will do it, no matter what."

He shoved his hat back and scratched his head. "I think so too. I need to talk to some bankers, but not in my army fatigues. I need to find some clothes. Never needed them fighting the damn Germans for four years." It was damn frustrating, and he didn't know where to begin.

"So, buy you some. I know you can do anything. Look at those horses."

"You're right. I'll buy some Levis, one white long-sleeved shirt, and a pair of boots. Might as well get me some khaki shirts to work in while I'm at it."

Jones came out of his *jacal* and greeted them. "Gaines said if he could help you, to call him anytime."

"He ever say what I owed him for doing it?"

Jones shook his head like the whole situation was too much. It still looked sort of iffy that he would stick with Mark on this deal. Dang it. He could use him as a partner. He'd keep working on him.

Alma hopped down off the wagon and faced Jones. "You have supper fixed?"

Jones chuckled. "Not yet."

She sniffed. "I bet you'd eat crackers first."

He never answered.

She went off laughing and tucking her long dark hair off her face. "I'll cook something."

Feeling a little better about Jones, he unhitched the team and the spare horses and put them up. When he finished, he went to where Jones was squatted, whittling on a stick.

"You still thinking about that ranch?" Jones asked him.

The small nod told enough. "I'm going to go look for a banker."

"Good."

His tone sounded promising. "I want to wash up some. She'll have some food soon."

"You remember what I told you? How do you think she just made that truck appear?" Jones nodded enough for the eagle feather to rustle on his hat. "You will see."

***

Two days later, dressed in a white starched shirt with a small western string tie, a pair of Acme boots and Levi's, and a straw hat in hand, he approached the First Arizona State Bank. He had a memorable meeting with a stern-faced loan officer named Arthur Bloom.

After Mark explained his entire plan for acquiring the Hancock Ranch, the man bent over his desk and told him, "The bank is not interested in investing in ranch mortgages. We are looking at the expansive housing boom beginning to start in the valley. Would you like to secure a government-sponsored loan on a house in Phoenix or Mesa?"

"No, thank you." It was hard to pay attention to this pot-bellied banker with the low hum of people talking in the busy bank. But he got the gist of it. He'd get no money here.

His next stop was the Sun Bank. The meeting was much like the first one. They didn't make ranch loans either. When he finished, he considered going to Phoenix to check with those banks, but when he fled the last one, he had lost his excitement for the task. He went to a phone booth and asked for Sam Cline's phone number. The Bell operator placed the call and told him to put a nickel in the box.

"Mister Cline there?" he asked the girl who answered the phone.

"Who may I say is calling?"

"Mark Shaw."

Silence, then she came back. *"May I ask what is the nature of your business with Mister Cline?"*

"I have a twenty-thousand dollar deal I want to share with him."

Silence. Behind him a wagon rattled by, followed by a Model A that made so much noise Mark plugged his other ear. This Cline fellow was well known for his big deals. Surely this one would appeal to him.

A man's voice roared in the phone, startling him. *"What's this bullshit about twenty thousand dollars?"*

"Mister Cline, Mark Shaw here. I have a deal that could make you some big bucks, and some for me, too."

"Well, what is it?"

"A ranch that's been abandoned. Both the owners died and the cattle have not been worked in five years."

"How many damn cattle?"

"They say lots."

"Who says lots?"

"A neighboring rancher who knows cattle."

"Who in the hell has it?"

"Some lawyer has it."

"Why call me?"

"'Cause I know you like to make money."

Cline paused. *"Where you at, boy?"*

"I ain't a damn boy. Now listen, I've been over there killing damn krauts for near five years. I'm home now and I'm looking to get myself a ranch. Now, if you want in on it, fine. If you don't, say so and I'll make someone else a pile of money." He bit his lip and waited, hardly breathing.

"Where can I call you back?"

Whew. A good first step. "I don't have a phone."

"Send me a letter with all the information."

"Let's talk, man to man. I'm not illiterate, but someone is going to find this deal, and you and I will both lose it."

"I don't buy blind horses unseen."

"I don't expect you to."

"I'm on the third floor of the City Bank building on Main Street. When can you get here?"

He had no intention of running down there. "Thirty minutes." He knew damn good and well where that man's office was located. The silence got on his nerves. Was the man changing his mind?

A rustling of papers, then his voice came back on the line. *"I'm going to dig up some property maps. This better not be a damn hoax. I don't have time to waste on bullshit."*

"I heard you. See you then."

Cline hung up the phone.

He held onto the phone, staring out of the phone booth, then grinned and whooped. The operator came back. *"May I assist you, sir?"*

"No, ma'am. Thanks." He hung up the phone. Three ladies waited in line to use it, all acting like they owned the danged thing. He barely slid out between the booth and a huffy woman.

He excused himself as she glared, pushed by him, and said under her breath, "Some people have no manners."

He was so excited he really considered saying something smart-alecky to her, but he refrained.

Still coming off a high from his conversation, he went down the block to the Five and Dime soda fountain. When he walked in, the fragrance of ladies'

creams and new cloth slammed him backward in time. He had been in here as
a little kid, buying two-for-a-penny candy when his old man got paid, and later
with Francine, a girl in school who gave him the eye in class. He hadn't thought
of those days in years. It was good to be home, but he hadn't really taken time to
think about what life here would be like. That was all in the past and this was the
present. Today he sidled up to a red stool, sat, and ordered an ice-cold chocolate
malt. The thick drink came in a tall glass and the cute teenager set a metal mixer
tube that had a lot more in it on the counter.

"Twenty cents." She leaned on the counter and gazed at him, her long blonde
hair swinging.

He gave her a quarter and told her to keep the change. She smiled with lipstick all over her mouth. "I ain't seen you in here before."

"I've been gone four or five years in the Army."

"You got any medals?"

"Yeah, a whole shoebox full."

"Wow. You really look like a soldier."

Had he ever been that young? If so, he couldn't quite recall it. He laughed.
"In these clothes?"

"No, but you stand tall. What are you going to do next?"

"Go buy myself a ranch."

"Where?"

"Bloody Basin."

"I never heard of that place. What's your name?"

"Mark Shaw."

"Nice to meet you, Mark. My name is Carol. I get off at five."

"Thanks. Maybe someday. Today I have to close a deal."

"I've got a customer and have to run. But I work here all the time. Remember
my name. It's Carol."

She walked away, hips swaying. How did women just know to do that? He'd
never figured it out, but maybe they were born cute and flirty.

The straw in his malt made a sucking sound, interrupting his thoughts. He'd
finished it without barely tasting a single swallow, only thinking of the pretty
girl and his ranch. Right now, he didn't need the one but had to have the other.
Back out on the sidewalk in the too bright sun, wiping the sweat, he stared not

at the streets of Lehi but into the past. In Europe, it would be cold by this time of year. Shaking away the memory of echoing gunshots that hovered just over his shoulder, he hurried down the block and a half and went into the bank lobby. He took the elevator to the top where it stopped like a drunken bus driver. He waited until the doors parted and then stepped off.

Why did banks always smell hollow?

The sign on the frosted glass said, *Samuel Cline Enterprises, Salt River Land Company, Samuel Cline, President.* Well, old Sam had been home making lots of money while he'd been off in the mud, getting bloody fighting krauts.

He recalled, years ago, Sam coming around like a big shot in his black Lincoln coupe and talking to his father about what he wanted done on the farm of his they lived on. He bet the old man never even knew his name in those days.

A woman sat typing at a desk, the clickety-clack of the keys the only sound in the room. She looked up. "May I help you, sir?" She had drawn-on eyebrows and a thin face.

"My name's Mark Shaw. I have an appointment with Sam Cline."

"Mister Cline is talking to a client currently. Have a seat. When he finishes, I'll tell him you are here. There are magazines on the coffee table. It may be some time. This is a very important client."

"Thank you, ma'am."

He looked at the clock on the wall. Two-ten. How long would the old bastard stall him? Since his discharge, he didn't bother with clocks or watches. The sun was his timepiece and he felt secure enough doing that. By three o'clock, he'd read every dog-eared *Life* magazine and a chapter of a western short serial in the *Saturday Evening Post.* The cowboy was left afoot at the end of the chapter and his bucking horse ran off.

There were no later copies of the Saturday Evening Post there. He'd have to guess how the story ended.

The woman spoke into the silence. "Mister Cline will see you now. Please make your presentation short. He has another appointment in thirty minutes."

You just bet I'll make my 'presentation' short. Short enough to show how busy he was. He shoved through the door, hustled across the large office toward a white-haired man behind a large shiny desk with files neatly stacked on one corner.

"Mister Shaw. How are you today?" Cline didn't rise but shuffled at the files to show he was indeed an important man. He glanced up but offered no handshake. The chair he sat in squeaked. "Where do I know you from?"

"Officially, we've never met before. I've been away for over four years. I'm discharged now and heard about this ranch."

"A veteran, huh?"

"Yes, sir."

"Have a chair. I have a few minutes."

Mark took the upholstered-in-leather chair facing the desk and leaned forward. "A rancher from the Verde Valley gave me a ride down from Flag a few weeks ago. His name is Rough Cravens. He said the old folks who owned this place both died in a short span of years. Must have been before the War. Help's been short, and the place has sat vacant. Mavericks are running all over it and no one has had the labor to work it. He said lawyers have it and the heirs are in California and don't want it." He'd spouted all he could think of to tell the man, then paused, watched, and waited. Must've been enough.

Cline punched on his intercom. "Send Jim Burch in here with the land map he mentioned."

There was a large, polished wooden table and big leather chairs around it like General Ike had in his office in France when Mark got his big medal. Two men entered and went directly to the table.

Cline ushered a very excited Mark there. "Jim, this is Mark Shaw. He's looking at a deal up on the Verde."

The man under the visor looked to be forty and wore thick glasses. "Nice to meet you, sir." He didn't look up but put the large maps on the table. They looked very official. "I found the Hancock Ranch on this one, sir."

"Does it have a landing strip?" Cline asked.

"I doubt it," Mark said, looking at the Verde River snaking down through the land adjacent. It might be a helluva place to have a ranch. Plenty of water. Moderate elevation there, but it was not in downtown Mesa.

Jim had a notebook that he recited from, "The Hancock Ranch has six hundred forty acres of deeded land and a Tonto Forest grazing permit for three hundred mother cows. County property taxes have been paid. It belongs to the Hancock Estate and is still in the estate. Agent is Attorney Larry Hall in Mayer, Arizona."

"Have you ever talked to that son-of-a-bitch Hall?"

"No, sir." Mark wanted to bolt at his tone. Could Hall be some sort of crook?

"Well, let me tell you, he's an old crook. I guess if I was trying to live on a law practice in downtown Mayer, I'd have to steal too."

So, he was a crook. "Can he be dealt with?" Mark turned to look back at Cline for an answer.

"Anyone can be dealt with. We simply have to watch our tails. I have a pilot and we can fly over it and count cattle. Then we'll know more. Jim can make a smaller map and we'll see what it consists of and if there are cattle."

He wasn't exactly excited about flying in a small airplane, but it would be one way to see the ranch. This deal was moving forward so fast he felt like hanging on to something. From what he got from Craven on his ride through hell, the ranch roads, after all this time, might have been washed out by heavy rains. When no one went in or out for several years, that tended to happen.

"Meet us out at the Dutch Field about nine tomorrow and we'll look at the place from the air. Jim, you make a smaller map. We couldn't handle that large map inside my Piper Cub."

He knew the model—four seats. They scouted Germans in them. Three or four times he'd flown to see what the landscape ahead was like for his commander. He'd rather ride a bronc horse on a frosty morning. It wasn't as far to fall. But to see this place and make a deal, he'd ride the wildest bronc on the rodeo circuit.

"What time'll you leave here? My car isn't running." The lie slipped easily off his tongue. Was he letting these big shots affect the way he acted? He hoped not.

"Jim, pick him up here at eight a.m. I'll meet you two out at the field."

Cline punched the intercom. "Hazel? Call my pilot and tell him to be fueled and ready at nine tomorrow. We're going up in Yavapai County to fly over some ranch land."

"Yes, sir."

Cline turned back to him. "She'll take care of that, don't you worry. I take it that you're a stock man."

"Yes, I'll have my own remuda and have some Maricopas to ride with me that are real hands." That was exaggerating a lot, but Jones and Alma could find what he needed later. He had to act like he was up for this and knew his business.

"That would be good. I didn't think you could get any Indians to work. But you obviously know more about them than I do. Jim, don't forget to pick up our new associate, Mark here, in the morning. See you all out at the airport."

"Thanks." He shook Cline's hand.

Cline paused. "I've seen you before. But no matter. This sounds interesting. Thanks for the heads up. We will see what we can do. Good day, sir."

"I can find my way out," Mark told him and left.

The elevator closed in on him going down the short distance. He wanted to throw his hat in the air. He wanted to leap out of this clanging, rattling, creeping elevator and hug every woman on the street. Finally, the doors opened and he headed straight for the street. Outside, he inhaled the exhaust-filled air. At least he was outside and could breathe. He stopped a half block away to get his bearings. Still feeling nauseated and antsy, his escape was slowly evaporating the fears of his last frantic moments in Cline's office. While lots of his fears and disruptions were easing, the war damn sure wasn't over. Not for him.

Alma waited at the Indian Pony Parking Lot with her buckboard and two horses. He laughed at the sight of her and the rig in the bleeding sunset. What would his new partner think if he knew about his mental problems? That he was living in sin with a full blood not two blocks from his fancy third-story suite, with his intercom, big table with leather chairs, and a well-perfumed secretary who wore nylon hose. They made a small rasping sound when she walked, rubbing together at her thighs.

Alma had a fire built and was ready to cook hot dogs for supper.

Bent over, he kissed and hugged her. He shook his head over all the happenings. "It's been a long day."

"I bet it has been that. You do any good?"

"Banks are not any help. But Sam Cline, a rich man, is taking me flying over the ranch to see what we can make out. He called me one of his associates before I left his office. I believe we have ourselves a ranch. But we have to be careful not to celebrate too soon."

Her eyes opened like saucers and she gasped. "You are going to fly?"

"Yes, why?" That's all she got out of his news? He laughed, grabbed her around the waist and whirled her round and round. "Woman, I'd fly without an airplane to make this deal."

"Are you afraid?"

"No. I've flown before." Hell yes, he was afraid. Of a lot of things. Of dealing with people like Cline, of making promises he might not be able to keep, of spending someone else's money on what might fail. But he'd never in a million years admit it out loud. You had to stand up, be brave, and face anything that frightened you. Just like in the war. No man ran from what scared him. He ran to it and cut it down.

"Oh, my. I wouldn't sleep tonight if I knew I must fly tomorrow."

He simply laughed and hugged her shoulder. "I hope I've made a deal." He had to tamp down his expectations till something happened, but everything was looking hopeful.

"I hope so, too." She wrinkled her thin nose. "I don't like being in town all day."

"Neither do I. Neither do I." Chills ran up his spine thinking of those moments in Cline's office. How he shook with hope, how bad memories of the war threatened to overpower him before he left Cline's office. He'd much more liked to have been riding his new sorrel horse in the desert.

She shook her head, then wrapped the blanket tighter. "I'm glad I don't have to fly tomorrow."

How strange that she could only think of her fear of flying. Maybe it didn't occur to her how important getting Cline's backing to buy this ranch was to him. He wasn't exactly thrilled about flying, but it went with the deal and was the least of his worries.

Funny how good the hot dogs tasted when you knew it wasn't all you had to eat. Sitting beside her in the parking lot, discussing their future, he couldn't have been happier. All he had to do when he wanted something was want it bad enough to work like the very devil to get it. First Alma, then the five wild ponies, and now backing to buy a ranch was in his grasp. It was like a dream. Sometimes he was afraid he might wake up to find himself in a foxhole, dodging bullets and mortar shells. Best he didn't get started thinking about stuff like that. He was home safe, had a woman he loved who loved him. Why dwell on the past? It had come and gone, and he'd dealt with it. If Cline turned him down, he'd deal with that too.

But he sure hated to think that might be the outcome of tomorrow's trip up to Bloody Basin.

"Time to go to bed." Alma's voice interrupted his train of thought.

He crawled under the wagon and into his bedroll next to her, falling asleep with hopes of success. This would not fail. He wouldn't let it.

4

CASEY HARWOOD SAT IN THE pilot's seat, wearing a leather helmet and a white scarf around his neck. Over the two-way radio, he received clearance from the tower to take off. Mark did his best but couldn't understand the words through the static.

He sure hoped the pilot could.

The plane soared off the runaway over the vast citrus groves surrounding the former training base for the Dutch military flyers during the war. The take-off left Mark's stomach somewhere down on the landing strip. Tilted on one wing, the plane turned and headed north toward Bloody Basin. Maybe, if he didn't look out the window, it would help. He tried concentrating on the maps Jim held, but the way they were rolled, he couldn't make out much. One thing was for sure. He was glad it was a sunny, windless day and the air wasn't bumpy. Still, he wished they were all on horseback, even though it would take a good three days to get up there.

He stared at the back of Sam's head. He wore a snap-brim felt hat. Mark shared the rear seats with Jim and his many rolls of maps. When the plane reached altitude, Mark leaned forward to better see all the farmland and irrigation canals that fed water to the valley. To his right were the McDowell Mountains and Red Rock that Harwood soon smoothly turned the plane to fly over. Everything passed under them.

Strange to view the land they had beat their butts raw riding over to capture the ponies. Seeing it from up here, it looked smooth and flat, but he knew better. There were rivulets cutting through it, and here and there a hole that could easily break a horse's leg. But even so, he'd much rather be riding flat out on that big wild bay they'd caught than floating around up here.

The river glistened in the sunlight, a twisted ribbon shining like a diamond necklace, cutting through the dust and rock formations. It was impossible to envision the some six hundred acres of what he hoped would soon be his ranch.

Harwood was dressed in starched tan pants and shirt, with his cigarette holder and his knee-high brown English riding boots. He could have been Clark Gable. Mark expected him to speak with an English accent, but his was Southern instead. He could hardly wait to tell Alma about this guy.

"My plan is to fly straight up the Verde Watershed. When we get close to this ranch, we can circle and look at it from a lower elevation," Harwood said.

"How many hours of safe flying do you have?" Cline asked him.

"Several thousand, sir."

"The insurance on his flying is so cheap compared to Jim or I, we couldn't afford to fly it ourselves. Can we, Jim?"

"No, sir."

Mark didn't miss that Jim almost crossed himself in gratitude. His mind remained on the motor's hum. When it quit—if it quit—they'd go down like a rock, considering this was not a place like Oklahoma or Texas, where you could land just about anywhere. Coming home on Route 66, he'd rediscovered how flat the land in that country was. Real boring. Nothing like here where the levels changed with almost every step.

"Okay, we're coming up on your ranch. You can see it off to the right." Harwood tilted the plane a bit, so they could see better. Mark wished he wouldn't do that. He could see perfectly well flying flat.

He and Jim both leaned forward to see.

The ranch headquarters looked a little rough.

"How will we get in there with no roads?" Though he hadn't meant to, he'd spoken the question aloud. They'd have to ride in or use the wagon until a road could be put in.

"Won't take long to solve that if the place proves out." Sam Cline didn't sound too worried about a little thing like roads.

Harwood made some swoops on the place, so they saw the corrals needed repairs. Herds of white-faced cattle looked fat but threw their tails over their back and ran like hell from the plane's low passes. If only he could be with them, Mark would gladly ride one of their backs to get out of this damn plane.

"Hurrah, we've got cattle," Cline said. "But they look wilder than Billy goats."

Harwood made another pass over the place and a fat twelve-point buck mule deer went hopping up through the junipers. There was food there, too. The man swooped around and flew west toward the Bradshaw Mountains. Then he came back over the ranch and the Verde.

"Enough, Mister Sam?"

"I've seen enough." Cline nodded and looked back at Mark. "How in hell are you going to get in there?"

Mark swallowed hard. "Horseback. It'll be a lot easier ride than this has been."

"Take it you don't like flying much. But can you run a dozer?"

"I've run several models."

"You know they'll have lots of them for sale, now that the war is over and they're cheap as surplus. We may need one up here, so I can eventually drive up to your front door in my Lincoln."

"I'd like that. Hell, we can even build you a runway with one of them." Drive up to my front door? Mark sure did like the sound of that.

"That would be the way. Right Harwood?"

Harwood kinda prefaced his reply. "If it isn't too rough. I can put this baby down there."

Damned if he didn't even sound like Gable when he said baby.

One last look at the log house with some shakes missing, fallen-in corrals, and sheds. Maybe more work up there than Jones wanted to do—if indeed Jones was his partner. The man seemed on the fence, balking at the hard work ahead. But he felt much better listening to Cline and Harwood discuss what might soon become his ranch. Or at least *partly* his.

Then that fool Harwood stalled the engine and Mark's stomach flew right out the window. His toes curled on the floor and he shook with fear. Back in the war, he'd figured once he got home he'd never be afraid of anything again. Well, he'd got that wrong. They were going to crash, sure as the world. Then the pilot switched gas tanks and Mark held his breath until the sputtering engine caught again.

Whew.

They were halfway back to Mesa and the flying field before his heart hit an even beat. Jim must have felt the same way. He mopped his sweaty face with his kerchief. He shook his head at Mark and then mouthed the words Harwood couldn't hear over the roar of the plane's engine. "That bastard does that every time to show off. I could kill him."

Those were nearly Mark's sentiments, as well, but killing the pilot wouldn't be the smartest thing he could do at the moment. So he did his best to relax until the damned fool landed the thing.

"Listen, Shaw, I'm going to talk to that lawyer, Larry Hall, about some other deals and slip in some questions about this ranch."

"Sounds good. Anything I need to do?"

"Call me next week, like Tuesday. Now I want to try and make us a deal where you and I can make some money. If I can't do anything, you may need to go up there to Mayer and dicker with him for us. Don't worry. I have enough money to buy half of the ranches in Arizona, but we'll need to see how to buy it for the lowest dollar so we can really make some money."

"Yes, sir." Mark swallowed hard. Was this really going to happen? "Is morning or afternoon the best time to call you?" He managed to sound calm and collected but it wasn't easy.

"Midmorning Tuesday. Where are you at?"

"Lehi."

"I have a notion, Shaw, that we'll be owning this ranch before much longer."

"Thanks. That's good to hear." Mark slumped back in the seat. Now Clark Gable needed to land this bee-bomber so he could ride back to Mesa and find Alma. Then they'd go home in her wagon, break horses, and he could entertain her with stories of his death-defying airplane ride. She'd get a kick out of that. But not much more of a kick than he'd got.

Dang, he'd be glad when this thing was on solid ground again.

———

WHEN HE FINALLY CAME TO join her on the horse parking lot, she stood waiting for him, wrapped in her blanket.

"We have a partner in the ranch deal. Let's go home and break horses."

"What was the plane ride like?" She smiled big, waiting for his answer as he picked up the harness to hitch her team.

"Spooky as hell. I'll tell you all about it tonight when we bed down at Jones's."

She ran over and hugged his arm. "I thought so. I would never have gone."

He pulled out on the road to Jones's place. Though it would take a few hours to get back, with no trouble he could make it in time for supper. With a lot on his mind, he was careful to check traffic. He started to pull out on the Lehi Road when some fool dodged around him to beat an oncoming car. The miss was so close, he gripped the reins and caught his breath, doubling his fist and shaking it. Whew, that was a near miss.

It took him a few minutes to stop breathing heavy. If this town kept growing so fast, they might have to put in traffic lights to put an end to things like what had just happened.

At the Lehi Store, he pulled in so Alma could pick up some supplies. After that, it was a short drive on home. Well, short compared to the drive up to his new ranch. Sitting out there on the seat of the spring wagon, he grinned like a fool. Tried out saying it. "My new ranch." Not bad. "Our new ranch." Much better. With luck, if Dirty Shirt was willing, there'd be four partners in this venture. A lot of work and, if Cline was right, a lot of reward, moneywise.

Alma returned, and he left off wishful thinking to jump down and help her load the supplies. The sun had set, and shadows walked across the land when he pulled up at Jones's place.

The Indian came out and leaned on the doorframe with his arms folded. "You talk to a banker?"

"Yes, and we flew over the place in his plane this morning. He's working on buying it right now." Arms full of supplies, Mark followed Alma and Jones into the *jacal* to store them away.

"Holy shit." Jones shook his head in disbelief. "You hear his words, woman? He flew over it. Did you go?"

"No, I have no wings. We were not meant to fly like birds."

Jones laughed. "I agree. What if we sell that stallion?"

"Why is that?" He helped Alma store sugar, flour, cornmeal, and beans while Jones lolled nearby.

"A man came by this morning. Aft Corning. He says he would give three hundred dollars for the stud. I say I can't sell him as he is only half mine."

"You can get three hundred for him, you better sell him."

"Good, he's getting your friend to haul him tomorrow." Jones smiled big. "I thought you'd think like me."

Busy working over her fire, Alma laughed. "Why did you even ask him if he wanted to sell it?"

Jones frowned at her. "I was on my best behavior."

"Oh, Dirty Shirt, you don't have none of that."

He ignored her. "When will we go up there?"

"I can't tell. But he is working on it. I think when the horses are broke to ride, we can go and see it."

"What does it look like?"

"Run down, but you can't tell much more than that flying over it that fast."

"Is it cold up there?"

"Not sure, I didn't get out to look around. But I expect it's about like here."

"No. One winter I was in Flag and nearly froze my fingers and toes off."

Mark laughed. "Come on and help get the horses put away."

Jones followed him and together they unharnessed the team and turned them in the corral to roll in the dust.

"That is way higher. This is down on the river. Let's go in. She'll have supper fixed soon."

Jones followed him, not hushing up. "You hear him, sister. He don't care if we freeze our asses off."

"Maybe you will need a wife for a stove?" She glanced toward the men with a big smile on her face.

"You find me a big fat one. She'd be warm."

"No, she'd steal all the covers off you to keep herself warm."

"Oh, damn, I can't win for losing." Jones laughed until he was bent over.

Mark stretched his back muscles, seating himself on a cottonwood log.

Those two sure did like to banter about anything. He hoped she hurried up cooking their meal. They could argue all night and then into the next day, still trying to get ahead of the other one. He shook his head in wonderment. Twelve hours earlier ahe'd been listening to the hum of the Piper Cub, now hearing his woman and partner trading jokes. What a world he lived in.

"I need to go get my saddle from Dad." Mark gestured toward Alma who cooked tortillas over the fire. She always rode bareback, which made him wonder what had happened to Jeff's saddle. She had it when they met up the first time, 'cause he saw it in her wagon, looking all shiny with soaping. He might ask her tonight after they crawled in their bedroll. Right now, he needed to satisfy Jones about the ranch deal, make him see what a good deal it would be for all of them.

Jones settled down nearby and stared at Mark. "You think you'll get it? The money, I mean."

Mark shrugged, played with a stick in the dirt by the fire. Supper smelled good and he was hungry. She was a fine cook, a better helpmate. How soon he'd begun to wonder what he would do without her. Life was funny.

It'd be hard to round up those wild cattle without Jones to help. He was one helluva cowboy for an Indian. Yet should he try to convince him to come in on it? His dad and Sam weren't exactly buddies. They'd had some problems back when Dad was a sharecropper for Cline. Being a kid, he wasn't sure exactly what it had all been about. Still, he didn't want to do this without Jones. Cline was not a philanthropist, but he might be the route for him getting a ranch manager's job and even maybe a partial owner of that place. He sure hoped he wouldn't hear any artillery rounds or machine guns burping in that isolated country. He really hoped Dirty Shirt would come in on a partnership should Cline offer it.

Maybe when Gaines came to haul the stallion for Corning, he could find out if there was a way in to the ranch. They'd need a decent road to get the trucks in there to haul those cattle or else have to trail drive them out.

Supper was finally ready. His thoughts trailed away when she brought him a plate of hot beans, warm tortillas, and fried bacon.

After they ate, she apologized. "I'm sorry I was so slow. I'm kinda tired. It's been a trying time for me. I was no help." She was weary from all their traipsing around, as well as waiting on him. But there was more to it than that. When he held out his arms, she fell into them and cried.

"Oh, I love you, but I simply can't forget Jeff. I can't accept that he died over there. Do you understand why?"

What had brought this on? She hadn't mentioned him in a long while. "I'm sorry. I didn't know you were still mourning him. What can I do?"

"I saw a calendar at the Lehi store and remembered he was killed a year ago today. It made me think of him all over again. I don't mean to be this way, but I did love him so."

He had no idea she had still felt this way and he felt bad for her. But what if she couldn't forget her first man for him?

He held her close, not knowing what to say. Hoping it was only the anniversary of his death that made her so sad. He couldn't lose her, surely, he couldn't. Was there always going to be something to worry about? In the war, the one thing was worrying about getting killed. Now it seemed every time he turned around it was something new to plague him.

"I have not been lying to you. You have stayed with me, been good to me. It is just so hard." Pressed hard against him, she broke down in tears.

"Come with me, Alma. I'll hold you in my arms on the bed." He led her off to the sun-faded sidewall tent from war surplus.

He found little solace for her until she went to sleep in his arms. So many things she knew about people and getting along, but accepting Jeff's death was beyond her reach. He knew about something being beyond one's reach. Things slipped off the end of his fingers too—he only hoped this ranch deal worked. Maybe up there, she could reach what she couldn't find down here. He snuggled close to her and closed his eyes until sleep came to him as well.

The next day, an old, battered Ford approached. His wife Shelia crawled out—not someone he needed or wanted to see. Alma seemed better. Calm and quiet. He worried enough about her without this. A cocky-looking driver stayed by the car. He wore a white t-shirt and kept his cigarette pack rolled up in the sleeve.

Wearing a dress a size too big for her, she marched right up to him, her black pumps kicking up dust. "Mark, I want a divorce."

Maybe she'd gotten that dress from the Salvation Army. Her hair looked dry and frizzy, her skin dry. She wasn't taking care of herself, but he had enough to worry about without taking on her troubles. All he wanted was to be rid of her after what she'd done to him.

How could he ever have wanted this woman? "Go get one, then. I won't argue for you to stay."

"I don't have the money. It costs thirty dollars. I swear I ain't got the money."

"I'll go find some paper and you can sign that I gave you the money, 'cause I don't trust you with it otherwise. The two of you might go on a wild toot."

Jones found him an old calendar month that was blank, and he wrote on the back.

I swear that Mark Shaw gave me $30 dollars for our final divorce on this day, the 17th November, 1945, for that purpose.

Signed, Shelia Shaw.

After she signed it, she handed it back to him. "I hate that you done me like this, Mark. Made me come beg you for the gawdamn money. I thought you was a real man."

He leaned over toward her before he spoke softly. "Just go bed that guy standing over there by the car. You've probably done it before and that won't be the last time. Goodbye, Shelia."

"You gawdamn *bastard!*"

"Stay over there, big man." Mark pointed to the man, who'd pushed off the car and started over, ready to defend his beloved bed-warmer. "I can whip your ass one-handed, and I want you to take this woman out of my sight."

The guy finally opened his mouth to say something. "Come on darling, he ain't worth nothing."

Sheila left crying, her new man herding her into his old car. Before he got in on his side, he gave Mark a big finger.

Mark gritted his teeth and clenched his fists, resisting the urge to march over and mop the dirt with the man. The car backed around in a big cloud of smoke and dust, the rods rattling in the V8 as it tore out over the humps in Jones's driveway.

Good riddance.

Alma hung on to Mark and he slowly cooled down from the height of his madness. When he looked into her concerned face, he lifted her up and kissed her mouth. "I only hope she never comes back."

"She's going to have a baby."

"Hmm. Well, it damn sure ain't mine. I haven't touched that woman since before the damn war."

She began to sob. "I am so sorry."

Now he'd made her sad again. "Aw, don't cry for me. I don't want you sad anymore. I love you." He hugged her again, ashamed she was so upset over his silly little problems. Sheila was nothing when compared to the loss of her husband.

Jones rose to his feet. "We better get these damn horses broke. If we get a ranch like you described, we damn sure will need every one of them."

"And every one of us, too." There he went, speaking his thoughts out loud.

Good thing Jones spoke up. It changed the subject and soothed his anger against the woman who meant nothing to him, not worth the wasted thoughts. Time to walk away from the past for good. Forget the war and his so-called wife and look to the future. It was bound to be better.

For him and Alma and Jones.

Holding Alma with one arm, he reached toward the Indian, as if to shake hands in a pact. "We partners?"

Jones eyed his outstretched hand, then stepped forward and took it. He held it tight and looked at him square on. "Partners." A pause and a big grin. "But that won't keep me from grousing about all the hard work."

Alma sniffed, then a laugh built in her chest and burst out. Mark joined her and soon all three were hee-hawing and holding each other in a tight circle. Mark sobered first, then Alma leaned against him and took a deep breath. Jones dragged out his bandana and wiped away his tears.

"This day didn't start out well, but we can change that." Mark picked up a few sticks of wood and tossed them on the coals. A flame leaped up, then another. "I don't know about you two, but I could use a cup of coffee and a good breakfast before we get busy breaking those wild ponies. What do you say?"

Alma fetched the frying pan. "I will warm the tortillas and fry some bacon if you will gather me a bit more wood."

Mark headed away from the *jacal*. "Wait for me, partner. I'm on my way."

Alma called after them. "Now you truly look like partners."

Mark waved an arm in the air. "That's what we are. All three of us." The day that had begun so lousy was beginning to look fine, one he could look forward to.

With a light step, he followed Dirty Shirt to a stand of juniper with a good supply of dead wood scattered about. Together, they picked up branches until their arms were full.

"That's a fine woman you have there."

"Don't I know it. You ought to get you one. They're good to have around, purty to look at, nice to hold. But make sure she can cook, or you might starve, the way you wrangle meals."

"I ever decide I need me one, I'll make sure and take your advice."

Mark chuckled. Good to be joking around again. This was all going to work out just fine. He had a hunch about that.

5

WITH BREAKFAST OVER, IT WAS time to break the wild ponies. Mark and Jones would go at it while Alma cleaned up camp and started a pot of *frijoles* for dinner. Leaning on the fence where they kept the horses, he glanced back at the *jacal*. Alma came out carrying a basket of clothes and headed down to the river. Her black hair hung in a braid against the colorful yellow blouse. In a skirt of blues and reds, she looked like a rainbow in the bright sunshine.

He was really home.

Here he would build himself a ranch. He might ought to pinch himself—make sure it wasn't a dream.

Oh, it was real all right, and Cline was a good choice to get this done. He had a reputation for being honest. Down in his gut, Mark needed it to happen. Needed to have a new life with Alma, and Jones as well. They were a fine fit, the three of them, each one doing what the other couldn't.

Horses whinnied and cut up behind him. He turned to make a choice for the first ride of the day. Dang, it felt good—the smell of horses and dust, the sun turning hot on his back, the thrill of the ride. He whirled his lasso into a circle, chose the high-stepping sorrel to start, and dropped the loop easily over its neck. Despite its wildness, the horse pricked his ears at the sound of Mark's voice while he eased the saddle onto its back.

"Easy there, boy. You and me, we're gonna have us a time, but you'll settle."

Rubbing the quivering neck, he placed a boot in the stirrup, easing his right leg over the sorrel's back and coming down into the saddle. Taking a good grip with both knees, he prepared for the explosion. Before going off to shoot Germans, he'd done this for a living. Hell, he'd done it for fun, when he wasn't picking cotton. Hooting and hollering while the crowd cheered him on—astride a stick of dynamite ready to explode. Waiting for the buzzer, knowing he'd made the eight seconds aboard chained lightning, and the crowd was going wild.

Now, it was different. Pride in what he had done so far, and hope in what was coming, rode this blamed crazy pony with him. Leaping high, coming down stiff, kicking out hind legs, the horse did everything he could to get rid of that burr stuck so good to his back. Nothing worked, so he slowed, trotted a ways, shook his head, and snorted in defeat. Trotting round and round, head held high, he acted as if the whole thing was his idea.

"You done good, you done fine." Mark rubbed between the flicking ears and rode a while till the animal knew for sure who was boss. After a while, he dismounted and slipped the saddle off.

One hand on the taut flank, he stood there a minute, gazing down at the river where Alma washed clothes. Sunlight danced across the water, making a halo around her. Dang, he felt good. Under his breath he chuckled. He'd already told the world he felt good, but it didn't hurt to repeat it. He straightened, turned, and picked out his next ride while Jones took a round with a sweet little dun.

That evening, they sat around the fire eating *frijoles* and tortillas and drinking black, scalding coffee right off the fire. Finishing her plate, Alma rose, dipped it into steaming water sitting on hot coals and moved to take the wash off the bushes where she'd hung it that morning.

"What about the big red?" Jones poured himself some more coffee to wash down the last of his supper.

"Tomorrow, I reckon. It'll take both of us, not like settling down one of the young'uns. They ain't got all their wild spirit yet. But him?" He shook his head in admiration. "He's greased lightning."

Jones nodded. "You on his back?"

The man knew Mark yearned to ride that red stallion. He'd made no bones about it, so there'd be no argument. That night, lying beside Alma snuggled into one bedroll, he went to sleep thinking about that horse. Not guns or battlefields or death, just that big wild horse and having it between his legs.

He woke up as the sun lightened the sky to the east and lay there for a while, watching blue tinges come alive above him. He eased out of the bedroll, careful not to wake Alma. Relieving himself in the brush, he imagined all the days ahead of them. Humming, he fastened his britches and gathered an armload of wood for the day's fire. Dropping it beside the glowing coals from the night before, he grabbed a bucket and went down to the river to get water to put on the fire for washing up after breakfast.

Living out like this suited Mark okay, but he'd be glad when they built a proper house and moved up on the ranch. Alma stirred and joined him, laying kindling on the coals. He leaned toward her and gave her a kiss.

"What will you do today?" She slid the skillet onto a rock and laid bacon in it.

"Gonna break that big red stallion."

She shook her head. "He is a big one. So pretty, but so mean."

"He ain't mean, just wild. We'll take that out of him without killing his spirit. Jones is good at that. He talks to horses and they hear him."

"Oh, and so the horse will just do what you ask?"

Mark laughed. "Well, not exactly, but he will know that we don't want to hurt him, but simply to make him useful. He can still run when we want him to."

"You will be his master."

"Something like that, I guess."

Shaking her head, she went about preparing breakfast.

What was coming with the red horse wouldn't be any eight second joy ride. It would take both of them, him and Jones, to get this done. After breakfast, they got to it.

Left foot in the stirrup, Mark swung his other leg over and was ready for whatever the big red horse had to offer. Jones led him riding one of his stout horses. Still, it was no surprise when the wild-natured animal tried to buck him off. Jones had him snubbed tight enough on his horn so there was no head ducking allowed, and the snorting and kicking was short-lived.

It became an everyday ritual for him and Jones to get up at dawn to ride an unbroke horse snubbed to a tamed horse until all six were broke. Two of the horses were fine in no time. The others took more discipline. By about the fifth evening, it looked like they were about done. Six fine ponies stood eating hay in the corral, only spooking when startled instead of kicking up a fuss at every turn. They were good-natured, and Mark took to stopping to admire them while doing other chores.

There was wood to chop for Alma's fire, water to carry from the creek, and of course the tending of all the stock including cutting them grass every day. It was the beginning of a good life and Alma took to it well.

On Tuesday into the second week, he and Alma went to Lehi where he made the call to Cline from the pay phone outside the store.

The man came on. *"Hell, Mark, that Mayer lawyer, Hall, is talking about the Hancock Ranch like it was the King Family's place in Texas that we're thinking about buying."*

"Really?" He frowned at Alma standing beside him looking anxious.

"Naw." Sam chuckled. *"He can't believe anyone wants it. We're going to buy it if you're damn sure you and them Injuns can make it a ranch. I don't know you, but I know you have fought like hell for this country and never run from fire. We'll be sixty-forty partners. But if you fail me, you lose it all."*

"I am not going to fail you, Mister Cline." A wagon rattled by, followed by two riders. Mark held a hand over his ear to hear what the man was saying.

"No, no. If we're partners, you call me Sam. I want you to go to Mayer for the signing of the papers when he gets them ready. For now, you go get a Kodak box camera and five or six rolls of film, go up there, and take pictures. When you get back, I'll have them developed. You take pictures of the buildings and everything pretty, too."

"You know we'll have to ride in there to do that?"

"I guess. Hold on." Sam spoke to someone else. *"No, we need two running bulldozers. If one breaks down, we can use it for parts. And some diesel fuel barrels."* He came back to the phone. *"Sorry, Mark. We found two bulldozers. We're going to need them. But, yes, you ride on up."*

"Yes, sir." He gazed at the brim of his cowboy hat. Bulldozers—wow. "Sam, I'll get some supplies and load up some pack horses to go up there. I expect to be gone over a week before I can call you again."

"Guess it's the only way we can do it. Get to a phone and call me next Monday."

"Sam, there aren't any phone lines up there."

"You're right. Come back before two weeks is up—like two weeks from today—and be ready to go sign those papers. Take those pictures and bring the rolls of film to me. And try to keep all your expenses written down. I'll reimburse you for them. Food and everything. Have you got a gun?"

"A Broomhandle Mauser pistol."

"Find a .30-30 rifle and shells. Buy one, borrow one, whatever. Hell, up there you might find a grizzly bear."

"Yes, sir. I'll leave in the morning for the ranch, take pictures, shoot a bear, and be back all in ten days or two weeks."

Alma startled when he said that. She mouthed, "A bear?"

He chuckled.

"Excuse me?"

"It's nothing, uh—Sam."

"Fine. Keep all the receipts. Buy that rifle. You got the money to do that?'

"I'll be fine on that."

"Good, good. Mark, you be careful up there. I'm counting on this working because you're my partner."

"It will, Sam."

"See you when you get back."

"Thanks—" But he'd already hung up. He put the receiver up and stood, a little shaken. He looked over at Alma. "Let's go sit down."

"You look about to faint. You all right? What was that about a bear?"

"It was nothing… at least I hope not. He was teasing. It's not that. It's that this is really about to happen. Hard to believe we're getting that ranch." He hugged her. "It's going to be a happy life."

"I sure hope so. Maybe if you shoot that bear we can have a big bear rug for the floor."

Both seated on the truck dock, he laughed and hugged her. "My God, Alma. I still can't believe how you came into my life that night in Mesa. This ranch is coming the same way. Like God delivered it to me, like he did you to me."

She smiled, pleased by his words. "What do we need to do?"

"Buy a box camera and ten rolls of film. Take pictures of everything up there.

We need to go do that for him and get back in ten days. We will own forty percent of the ranch. We have an expense account and I need to buy a thirty-thirty rifle." The words tumbled out like he couldn't stop.

"How come?"

"He don't want that grizzly bear to eat us up."

"I guess I don't either. Good idea to have a rifle." She doubled over laughing, "What will Jones do?"

"He can come along and be a partner, too. I won't cheat him."

"I guess it will work. He's having fun breaking horses." She slanted a glance at him. "And you are, too, I think."

She was sure right there.

A dust devil whirled across the road and between two buildings, churning up chips of wood and bits of gravel. Mark held onto his hat. "Let's start. I want a saddle for you. I can't go to Chandler on horseback to get mine from Dad, so let's buy one. We can charge our needs here."

Her feet became of great interest to her all of a sudden.

"What is it?"

"I did not mean to make you buy a saddle. That one of Jeff's. It made me miss him, so I left it somewhere."

"Is that what happened to it? I wondered. Don't worry. It was yours to do with as you pleased. I'm sorry you're still sad. Jeff was a good man and it's too bad he was killed in the war. But you have a new life ahead of you."

"I gave it to a man who had no money and a dumb little bony horse. Hard to ride bareback."

"That's a good thing to do. We have money to buy you a new one."

"You are not mad with me?"

"Of course not. You're my sweet girl. Don't worry a bit. Come on, let's get moving. We have lots to do and finding you a nice saddle is first."

Her eyes danced. "Buying all these things. I've never done anything like this before. It'll be fun."

He hadn't either, but he just smiled at her enthusiasm.

Mr. Wayne Pierson, who owned the store, came out on the dock to check on the weather. "Nice day." He nodded toward them. A short, stout man in his forties, he always wore a suit and tie and polished, low-cut shoes.

"You know Sam Cline, sir?"

"Yes, I do. Mister Cline owns several farms and cotton gins. Why's that?"

"As of ten minutes ago, I became his ranch partner. Alma and I need to go in by horseback and look at this ranch for him. We will need several things and we have his okay to charge our needs."

"A big job, is it? Well, congratulations. That's quite an increase in your work. My goodness. What can I get you?"

"A Kodak camera and ten rolls of film."

"I can have them here by five o'clock. What else?"

"A .30-30 rifle."

"I bought one a week ago. Will a used one work? It's been well cared for."

"How much?"

"Twenty-five?"

"That'll do. Put two boxes of shells with it."

"Come on inside. We can figure this out better on paper."

He took Alma's hand. "And this little lady needs to pick out a saddle. I'm sure you have some nice ones."

Mr. Pierson glowed. He was making a good sale and Mark could see he was happy about it.

It was no surprise to Mark that she chose a used saddle that had been well kept. Sitting in it, feet dangling above the stirrups, she rocked back and forth. "It is more easy to ride in than a new one that needs broke in."

He helped her down. "Then we will take this one."

After listing the other things they would need, they left the store. An hour later, Pierson sent them to a guy's place to pick up some packsaddles from a man who had sold them to the store keeper. His .30-30 and ammo in the wagon, they were to come back and pick up the rest in the late afternoon.

He took Alma's hand. "Want to go and get a soda?"

"Oh, yes! I have never had this soda."

"Well, you don't know what you've been missing."

In the Five and Dime, he went to the counter and ordered their sodas, choosing for her when she asked him to. He led her to a booth, sliding in on the red vinyl to sit on the same side as she did. He took a nickel from his pocket and set it on the table. "Put it in the jukebox. You can pick a song."

She studied the buttons for a while, then turned to him with an abashed look on her face. "I cannot read, so you will need to pick the song for me."

He cupped his hand under her chin. "That makes no difference to me. You are a fine cook and a good helpmate, so what does reading matter?"

He chose a Hank Williams tune for the offering and she patted her foot to the music until the sodas came.

Some of the people who came into the Five and Dime looked overlong at him and Alma. It was still not accepted by many to see mixed couples, but in Arizona, you saw it more because of the population of Indians. Mostly men with no family took what was referred to as squaws as wives or simply lived with them without marriage.

He and Alma were married, according to her, and so he accepted that as right and proper. He ignored the stares and kept talking to her to keep her from seeing it. What could really be wrong when they loved each other and helped each other? It hurt no one. He wanted to stand up and shout at those being so rude, but he held his temper. It would only hurt Alma.

Instead, he sat beside her while she drank her strawberry soda with a shudder at the first sip, then delight while she sucked it all down.

"Like it?" He couldn't help laughing with her when she finished. He had so much fun with her because she enjoyed even the simplest of experiences.

After they finished the ice cream treats, with time to spare, he took her hand to walk along the boardwalks up one side of the street and down the other, studying the offerings in every window. She spied a blue dress in a dress shop and stopped to gaze through the glass.

He stood beside her. "One day, after we have this ranch going, I'll bring you back here and buy you that very dress. It will look so pretty on you."

She covered her mouth and turned to him. "Oh, that is so sweet, but you do not have to do such a thing. We will need many other things for our house." Hand clenching her mouth, tears rolled down her cheeks. "My goodness. I did not mean... mean to say that. About us having a house on the ranch. You have not asked me to... I'm sorry."

He touched the top of her head, ran his hand down one of the long braids and held it, unable to meet her moist stare. Lord, he didn't like to see a woman cry. And especially didn't like to be the cause of it. He was sorry he had never said anything to her about being his wife, but now that he was to have a divorce from Sheila, perhaps he should. It was only right. Though it was frowned upon for a white man to marry an Indian, he didn't mind about that at all. She was beautiful and sweet and much nicer than his first wife.

"Listen to me, Alma. We will go back up there and take the pictures and let Sam do whatever he wishes. I think we will have the ranch and live there together. We will build a house and break horses and catch wild cattle and it will be a good way to live. You are with me and Jones if you wish, because you have helped every bit as much as any one of us. So, don't you cry or worry because you will have a place with us."

He couldn't bring himself to ask her to marry him yet, but it looked like he might ought to do that soon. They would talk some more about it once they brought the pictures to Sam and learned his plans. Surely, they could build a house and stop living outside with Jones. Now though, he had an idea.

"When we go up to the ranch, you will need a coat and hat. So, we'll go in the mercantile and see what they have."

She found an unblocked hat much like his, only tan instead of black, and a long-tailed black coat of wool. "This will keep me warm no matter if it does get as cold as you think."

He agreed and paid for the purchases out of his own pocket. Sam should not pay for this. He carried her package with the coat wrapped up inside, but she wore the hat, prancing down the sidewalk and singing in her Indian tongue. Some men stopped to watch but went on when Mark glared at them.

They got back to Jones's *jacal* after sundown, which came early that late in the year. He came out with a lighted lantern and looked over it all. "What did you buy?" He nodded toward her hat. "Besides that—which makes you look very... uh, white?"

She punched him on the arm. "Be quiet or I will not make supper."

"I suppose I could do that if I had to."

Ignoring their bantering, Mark explained the purchases. "Our partner bought this. I bought her a hat and coat, which you will agree she deserves. We need to get up there, take pictures for him, and get back in two weeks to close the deal. By Christmas, we will own a share in the Hancock Ranch. Maybe we can celebrate both events. What do you say?"

"I say it means more damn work." Jones grumbled and looked over the things. "You did good. You bought plenty of Oreo cookies."

They both laughed at him. Alma ran off to cook them some supper. Jones climbed down from his perch in the wagon, checking stuff out. He hung the lantern so she could see to make food by the lamp.

"Didn't I tell you she was a *bruja?*" he said in a whisper. "She found a truck. We found them horses. Now a ranch. Why, you even got rid of your dumb wife. You watch what I say, she has power."

Mark shook his head. "I don't give a hoot what you say about her being a witch. Have you been thinking about some boys to help us round up them cattle? Ones that will work." He hesitated a moment. "Jones, I need to know if you are staying to help. Yes, it will be work and hard work, and you grumble every time. Do you want in on this as a partner or not? I wouldn't want you to work yourself too hard."

Jones grinned. "You bet I do. Pay my grumbling no mind. It is just my way. And as for boys to help, if you can do it all on horseback, I can get a shitpot load of them."

"I want boys that will work. Carpenters to build fences and shovel horse droppings if needed too."

"May be a bit harder, but I can find them when we get back. How much?"

"We pay fifty and found. And the first thing we'll fix is a proper bunkhouse. One of the outbuildings can be fixed up for that. It'll keep them and us warm in the cold."

He nodded. "I bet we can get some good ones for that much."

"I bet we'd better. Now let's go eat. I figure she's got us some supper by now."

She had fixed them steaks and fried potatoes from the store to celebrate and looked elated about everything.

Later that night in their bedroll, she hugged him. "Thank you for what you told me today. It was a fine day, was it not?"

He put his arms around her. "Yes, it was indeed a very fine day."

Closing his eyes brought him thoughts of the new life they could have together, and about the ranch the three of them would build and share. The good times didn't follow him into his dreams, though. He walked in the valley of the shadows and woke in a sweat.

6

MARK, JONES, JIM BURKE, AND Alma left Lehi in the pack train on a frosty dawn. Jones took the lead, riding one of the new bay horses. Alma led the string of loaded horses seated in her newly-acquired saddle with the new felt hat Mark had bought for her, and she wore the black wool coat instead of her usual blanket. The horses they left behind followed until the end of the fenced pasture, then whinnied at the departing horses. They'd be alright. Jones had arranged for a couple of Maricopa boys to look after them.

Mark brought up the rear with the .30-30 under his right leg in the scabbard, his breath sending out misty puffs into the cold air. The sorrel horse did some sidestepping and dancing on his toes. Though prepared for him to buck, for the moment he only acted up a little. By the time they were back from up there, he'd be well broke. Meanwhile, he could hardly believe they really were going to his ranch in the mountains.

After they passed Fort McDowell the first day, Mark called a halt to consult the maps Jim gave him. He pointed to a spot ahead along the river where they could make camp.

"This looks like a good place. We're all tired and we've come far."

Jones agreed. "I have been up this river a long way. I know some trails we can take. But I have never been all the way to Bloody Basin."

"Don't worry. My maps will take us there... with a few detours along the way." Jim folded the map.

No matter the hardships, Mark was ready for just about anything. Nothing could dampen his fever for this trip. This might not be his ride to the ends of the earth like he'd planned, but he was making the ride of his life and by God he would enjoy it. He smiled at Alma, coming along and drawing the pack string along behind her. When they made camp, they didn't unload much so their leaving in the morning would be swift. Mark estimated four days to get them there by this route. They could only travel as fast as the slower pack horses.

That night in the bedroll, she whispered to him. "We saw several deer today."

"I know, but I may have to dismount to shoot one. Red might unload me if I shot one off him. When we get up there, I'll get us one."

She kissed him. "Good. That will suit me."

Day broke with clouds hanging in a bleak sky. The higher they climbed, the more apt they were to see snow. Some would be fine, but a lot could mean trouble fighting their way to the ranch. If he didn't think about it, maybe it wouldn't come. So, he shut his mind to all the bad possibilities. Eagerness to arrive and start his new life drove him on till he realized how hard he was pushing the big red horse, and thus the rest of the crew. His nose grew cold and he pulled a wool muffler up but kept on pushing.

"Why must we be in such a hurry? You'll wear out these animals." Jim's common sense brought Mark around and he reined in his mount. The man was right. He needn't be so anxious. It would do no good to kill the animals—or the people.

"It's another cold morning," Jones grumbled. "He's going to freeze us to death up here, little one."

Mark set a slower pace, taking his time to enjoy the surroundings.

Always the one to make light, Alma teased Jones. "You needed to bring that fat girl. She would keep you warm."

His laughter echoed in the canyon. "How did I forget her?"

Mark smiled at their banter. They were like kids. They were both okay for another day if they were arguing and picking on each other.

They reached a place midday that brought the first real trouble of the trip.

The trail rounded a bend and started a steep climb. Ahead was a steep mountain pass, way too steep to cross over with the heavily-loaded horses.

Mark studied the problem. "What do you think, Jim?"

"Let's stop here on these bluffs and have something to eat. We can look at our map and maybe see off down there to a better way."

After dismounting to munch on cold bacon and tortillas, Jim consulted his map. "Looks like, if we head over there through that cut, we can make it without much trouble. Unless there's been any landslides."

Snow continued to fall, but so far, the wind had laid off, and it wasn't piling up into drifts. That could soon block trails. Mark rose from his perch on a rock and leaned over the edge. "Yonder looks like an animal trail if we can work our way to it. We need to get down from here before this snow gets any worse."

Both Jim and Jones took a look and agreed they could lead the animals through the narrow cut and hit the trail that looked passable. It would be the easiest crossing since deer and elk often made such trails. The going was fine once they coaxed the nervous mounts around a fall of rocks nearly blocking the way. By the time they walked the animals through the dangerous pass and down the steep incline it was getting late, but they had reached the Verde.

Again, the three men had a meeting of minds. Mark usually gave in to Jim and Jones since they knew more about these mountains and rivers than he did. But if he didn't like something, he'd sure speak up. Alma kept silent most of the time when it came to discussions about keeping to the trail.

Mark didn't like that the only crossing they had was to ford the river. Best to always cross a river before making camp for the night. Never knew if a storm would hit upriver overnight, causing the waters to rise and make a more difficult if not impossible crossing the next morning.

Even though he was nervous about the crossing, he urged the long-legged bay into the water, bailing off halfway to swim beside the animal. He waded out, then returned the same way. It looked pretty hard for the pack animals and he sure didn't want to lose them and their packs.

He beckoned to Jones. "It'd be best if you, Jim, and I hand-lead each of the horses, then bring her across. I don't want to lose a horse or anyone to this river."

Jones nodded his agreement, as did Jim. They helped Mark with the back and forth crossings. It was hard going, but they finally made it. Tying the pack horses to some saplings, he went back for Alma, even though she had insisted she could do it alone. That was just like her, but he couldn't chance it. Once he led her horse up the bank to join Jones and the four pack horses, he breathed a sigh of relief.

Everyone was shivering with the cold. It was getting dark and Alma sat up against a big rock hugging herself.

"Come on, let's gather some wood and build a big fire. We can dry our clothes, get warm, and see our surroundings."

Jones eyed Mark and, always the jokester, let him have it. "Now, I'd say there's a great idea. Don't have a notion why I didn't think of it."

"Maybe your thinker froze." Alma never could resist razzing Jones. Their banter could be counted on to raise everyone's spirits.

"Taint all that froze, little gal." Jones simply couldn't let her get the last word.

They all went to work at what they each did best and soon had a big fire built to dry themselves and their clothing. Alma pulled some hot coals away from the huge flames, cooked their supper, and made a pot of coffee.

It was late when Alma took the hot beans and tortillas off the fire. Mark stirred his spoon around in his plate. Much as he liked beans, he'd be glad when they had something else to eat.

Worst thing was, they would have to make a crossing of the Verde again, for the river curled back around and would be waiting the next afternoon. He could only hope it would be an easier crossing. Once they made it, they would be close to the ranch. That was all he could think about.

———

THE NEXT AFTERNOON, THEY CROSSED back to the western bank of the curling river without any trouble. It was all he could do to keep from spurring his horse ahead to see what was truly—at least partly—his. He owned it in a way he'd never owned anything. He would run the ranch, see to the animals, the hands, the fencing and building. His excitement could hardly be matched. Eagerly, he rode out ahead, leaving Jim and Jones to see to the packhorses and Alma. He couldn't help it. He could wait no longer. Him, a cotton-picker from the fields. He now owned a place of his own. A real honest-to-God ranch.

And here it was. He swung off the bay and walked around, taking in the abandoned surroundings. There wasn't much sign of life, since the place hadn't been used by humans in years. Most all the fencing was down. They had crossed some a ways back. It made him sad to see the barbed wire stomped into the earth, pulled loose from posts, with more posts laying on the ground. What trails they'd found had been made by cattle or game. Nothing much to see yet. But there were buildings. He'd seen them from the air.

The rest of the crew rode up to where he had stopped to search for signs of life. He mounted, and they rode on in search of the ranch headquarters.

At sundown, the exhausted group finally found ranch headquarters and reined up. Mark's heart thumped under his rib cage like a large Indian drum. It looked like a real fine place to him, but he'd spent his youth in cotton picker shacks, so he might not be a good judge.

"It is gorgeous." Alma jumped down and threw her arms out.

Well, she wasn't much of a good judge either, seeing as how she'd lived. Still, the low set log home did not look as deteriorated as it had from the air. Jones called his attention to some shod horse tracks, a real surprise in the dirt.

"How long ago?"

"A week, maybe?"

"Probably someone checking on their own cattle."

Jones agreed, but not without a frown. Jim wandered about, checking on a bunkhouse that wasn't too dilapidated, considering no one had taken care of it for a long time. There was considerable work waiting for them.

They unloaded. The house had been closed, but pack rats had ruined the couch. One room had a bad roof leak, but the rest looked like someone left one day and never came back. Alma lit some candles they brought to see and cook by and they took the lantern to do some searching.

Inside the shop, under two inches of dust, they found a 1940 International pickup with only 7000 miles on it. Of course, the tires had rotted but with new rubber hoses, a fan belt, a battery, and tires, it should drive like a new one. Not bad, as hard as good vehicles were to get in these days of war-caused shortages. The '37 Buick also looked recoverable and had low mileage on the speedometer. After the Hancock couple died, the rest must have left the ranch, taking only their own things.

He followed Jones out of the shop and saw Alma must have recovered a kerosene lamp, 'cause the light in the house was much brighter than her candles were from before. It was getting real dark and hard to see, but he wanted to check yet another shed and did have the lantern. Where Jim had got to, he had no idea, but he was a grown man and wise in most ways.

In a shed in even worse shape, Mark was thrilled to find a once new Ford-Ferguson tractor in the same shape as the vehicles. Plows and other equipment were in there to farm with, including a three-point hookup to a mowing machine.

"I'd bet he had a patch of alfalfa he irrigated down here," he told Jones.

Jones nodded.

The tack room built on one side had six saddles. A little dried out but the room must have been rat proof. None had been gnawed on. Some fancy bridles marked the wall as well, though one was missing.

Mark rubbed a hand on the wall where it once hung. "There's no dirt on the space where the head stall once rested. These others are fitted with silver gal leg bits. Looks like they were made so the sides of the bit looked like some woman's bare leg. Kinda risqué looking, but these are expensive items. No doubt someone's taken off with one."

"They got that bridle recently, too." Jones said.

"I bet it shows up soon."

They walked back to the house to find Jim was there, helping Alma, who had built a cook fire in the fireplace.

"That bridle shows up, it'll be on some guy's horse's head." Jones chuckled.

Alma looked up from the skillet sizzling with bacon. "What's so funny?"

Mark went to hug her. "We've had a thief take a valuable bridle off the rack up here recently."

She frowned. "They sure came a long way to get one then."

He agreed. "We have a car, a truck, and a tractor. Need some work, but they should run."

Jones shook his head in despair. "You hear him say needs some work? This whole damn place needs lots of work."

"You would not be happy if you could not grumble about hard work. I think it is easy to find that here," Alma said. "But it will be a nice place when we get it fixed."

"How old will we be then?"

"I don't care," Mark broke up their repartee. "We own part of this place. In the morning, we start shooting film for Sam."

He liked the place. The fact that it had no road in or out didn't bother him in the least. It was his ranch, until it was straightened out. But if Sam did right by him, he'd have a stake to do something with when this place was sold.

Snow had passed them by come morning. Mark directing and Jones with the camera, they took pictures of everything—the parked vehicles, the bunkhouse, another pack rat den, the tractor. The list went on and on. Then the sagebrush-crowded field that Hancock once had in alfalfa with its diversion gate where he turned water in on it upstream. Mark patched the roof on the house and Jones took some pictures of cattle.

Mark was getting off the roof with a tar bucket he found to help seal the holes when Jones returned. Plenty of tools were in the shop to fix anything. Jim had gathered some up and hammering echoed from the bunkhouse.

"Looks like he's set to fix him a place to bunk. You ask him to stay yet?"

"Nope. He must've slept out there last night. Wonder how he stayed warm. Leave him be. We'll know soon enough, and he is working."

"I caught some pictures of cows and calves, but we must have a thousand bulls on this place—and not one of them is branded." Jones carried the camera real careful—like it was a crystal glass.

Mark gave him a wolfish grin. "That's what's going to pay for the ranch."

"How will we fix these rundown corrals?"

"We need those boys that you're going to hire to cut us poles on the mountain. You can snake them down on horseback."

"I'd damn sure rather pull them. They can cut them down."

"That's what I said, too. Give her the camera and let's check the pens out. We need to get back to Lehi. Sam'll be worried about us."

They walked over and seriously inspected the corrals. Some gates were gone, but the iron that hung them was still useable.

"We'll have to fix it before we start working cattle."

Jones agreed. "I better hire them boys."

"Yes." Mark sighed. More delays would stall his efforts to get on rounding up cattle. "I'm going to the house to make a list of things we'll need."

"I saw some signs, I think from a bear. I want to check it."

"Take the .30-.30."

The Indian shook his head. "No. I want to see how fresh they are."

"Up to you. Alma'll have lunch ready for us soon. Wouldn't do to let that bear eat you for dinner."

"That won't happen. I won't miss it." Jones waved at him and set out.

Mark reached the house and took a chair at the table. His notebook was open where he had written in several things to discuss with Sam.

"You found enough wrong to hire an army?" She laughed.

"We may need one—"

The crack of a pistol shot broke the serenity of the ranch, followed by someone yelling. Mark had the Winchester in his hands and ran out the back door. The shots and shouts came from west of the corrals where Jones had gone.

It was a voice he didn't recognize. "Get your ass out of here, you blanket ass Indian. You ain't squatting on this ranch—"

What the hell?

Mark located the demanding voice and stepped from behind a shed to see someone on horseback pointing a pistol at Jones.

The intruder shook the gun at Jones. "Gawdamn you! You ain't listening."

Mark aimed the rifle at the man. "I am. Now drop that gun or you're dead."

The armed rider turned and sagged in the saddle. Looking sullen, he lowered the pistol and dropped it to the ground. The decision saved his life, because Mark's trigger finger was at the pressure point on.

He edged closer, keeping the rifle on the newcomer. The man was about his age, tall and thin. "Who in the hell are you?"

"Gipson. Clay Gipson. And just who the hell are you?"

"Me and this Indian own this ranch. Where do you get off shooting at us?"

"I—I thought the Hancock family estate still owned it."

"Not anymore. Gipson, you came within an inch of dying just a second ago. Who gave you your authority to decide who can be here?"

"My family owns the next ranch over. I didn't aim to allow some gypsy Indians come and squat on this place. We plan to buy it when the estate's sold."

"You can't buy this ranch. It's not for sale. We *own* it. You aren't a deputy for this county, are you?"

"No."

"Then you were taking the law in your own hands?" He caught the flash of the bridle on the intruder's horse. "Did that bridle come from this tack room?"

"No, why?"

Mark nodded toward the horse. "I'm missing a bridle just like that from the inventory. Did you help yourself to one of those bridles?"

"No." The man looked around, nervous-like.

Mark gestured to Jones. "Go find him a bridle. I'm taking that one back. It matches ours, doesn't it?"

"Same bridle bit," Jones said, looking it over.

"Listen, there might be a mistake here," Gipson said.

"I think we know that. Jones, find him an old bridle to get home. Gipson, we're taking over this ranch. You're barred from coming here again, for any reason. Leave that gun on the ground—and if you ever threaten a member of this ranch again I'll come find you. I've spent the last four years killing Germans. One more dead bastard won't bother me none."

Jones came back and refitted the horse in an old bridle. He took Gipson by the collar. "Next time you shout at me, I'll jam a sock down your throat."

Gipson never answered him. He swung on his horse and charged away. Mark picked up the Colt pistol, then turned back to Jones. "We better hide those bridles before we leave—or take them with us."

"I could have killed him." Jones shook his head, casting a scowl at the retreating man's back. "He was damn sure about to start a new Indian war in Arizona."

"I don't blame you. We better go eat lunch."

Jones stared after the dust trail. "He ain't wasting any time getting out of here." The sounds of his hard-pressed retreat echoed over the mountains.

"I wonder if this pistol was stolen from the house, too?" He stuck it in his waistband. "We are going to have to watch ourselves out here."

"What was the shooting about?" Alma asked when they hurried inside.

"We met our neighbor."

"Who was shooting?"

Mark gestured toward Jones with a grin. "He didn't like Indians moving in here and squatting on this ranch."

"Huh?" She blinked in disbelief at him.

A wide-eyed Jim hustled through the door. "I was off down in a pasture when I heard the shooting. What happened?"

Mark told him while they sat down for lunch. He then asked, "You fixing up the bunkhouse?"

A spoonful of beans on the way to his mouth, Jim answered. "Hope it's okay. You said you were hiring men and I'd like to work for you up here if you don't mind. I don't get much work guiding folks around. Maybe someday, when tourists pick up again."

"Be fine with me. It's fifty and found. Like the others."

"Fine. I'll stay. Tell me something to do."

"Get that bunkhouse in shape while we're gone back down, unless you need to go back to Lehi for something."

"Nope, can't think of a thing." He put the beans in his mouth.

Mark turned back to the earlier conversation. He hugged Alma's shoulder. "Well, good thing that feller didn't see my pretty Injun. He'd a wanted to steal her away." He loved to tease her, and she liked it mostly. "He had also stolen one of the bridles. We got it back. Said he lives next door."

Jones laughed. "He nearly joined the dead Germans, too."

After lunch, Jones went out about his own business and left them alone. Jim went with him.

"Will he be any threat to me when you two are gone?"

He rocked her in his arms, standing in the main room. "No, he won't come back. Besides, Jim is staying. He wants to work for us. He'll be down at the bunk house if you need him."

She squeezed him. "I am so glad you brought me up here. I love this place. Lots of work but it is so nice. Only the magpies and blue jays to scold me."

He agreed with her, still wondering about Gipson. The worthless spoiled boy could be dangerous and backstabbing.

He held her close, sniffing the sweet wild smell of her hair. She fit so closely, tucked under his arm. How lucky could he be? He had a loving woman and a ranch. Two things he dreamed so hard about having after his discharge. He could hardly believe it had happened.

Reluctant to leave her, he kissed her on the nose and joined Jones working on the far corral to make it useable. They used some good rails from another one to fix a larger one. When they came back, they'd need them to hold more horses than they would hold at that minute. He dreaded going back to town, leaving this peaceful place, but he'd told Sam he would go with him to close the deal. They had more decisions to make, too. Hire two more cowboys, get some things packed in—lots to do.

"We better go back to Lehi tomorrow," he told Jones.

Jones nodded. "I may need to find a woman." He chuckled.

"You have a woman in line who will come up here?"

"I know a widow."

"You better warn her she has to ride in and out right now."

Jones agreed.

That afternoon they quit early, gathering everything needed to go back. They'd need to bring in lots of gear when they returned. Alma made a list of supplies. When she gave it to him, she said she had decided to go back with him. He told her it was whatever she wanted and so she busied herself to be ready to leave before dawn. Under the stars the next morning, they set out for their return. The air was frosty tinged, so they dressed for it in jackets, leaving at a jog.

Riding in the lead, he glanced over his shoulder. Dang, he hoped it was still here when they got back. You never knew what could happen off out here like this. Jim had a pistol and had reassured Mark he'd keep good watch over things. Mostly that Gipson fella could cause a heap of trouble if he found out they were gone. He'd best not, though. He'd just best not.

7

THE SECOND DAY OUT FROM the ranch, they pushed into Lehi and Mark reached the store's phone. He called Sam while Alma sat on a horse outside.

The banker sounded excited about their discoveries. *"Can you bring the film?"*

"I can be there at noon or so tomorrow."

"Leave them at the store tonight. I'll send someone to get them this evening. I'll have someone there to pick you up at the store in the morning at seven o'clock. You've done wonderful work. I imagine you're tired. In six weeks, you'll have a dozer up there to open the road."

"Good. If it'll run, we can do that."

"It'll run. I'm anxious to see your pictures."

"I'll be here in the morning."

"See you then."

"What did he say?" She handed him the reins.

"We need to leave the film here and someone will pick it up. They'll come after me at seven in the morning."

She took the sack of film from Jones, bounded off her horse, and took it inside. In minutes, she was back and in the saddle. They rode back to Jones's place. Totally weary, they dropped off their horses. The two-day hard ride back from the ranch had them worn out, as well as the horses. After the animals were unsaddled, fed, and put up, they dropped in their own beds, him and Alma in the tent, and Jones in his *jacal*.

Up before dawn, she cooked him some oatmeal and he shaved. Over his dress clothes—Levi's and white shirt—he wore a flannel-lined jumper and put on his best hat. She rode into town with him to bring the horse back.

Mark kissed her goodbye, not knowing when he'd be back.

"You be careful." She waved goodbye.

"That your wife?"

He nodded. No need to explain. She might as well be—hell, she was his real wife. If that last cheating woman of his had filed for a divorce, he should be free to marry her soon. Somehow, he doubted it though. She had probably blown the money he paid her. He might ought to've killed her.

Sam had things about the ranch all over the office, and his conference table was dotted with the photos. Mark looked at them, amazed. How in the world did he have them all developed overnight?

Sam shook his hand. "You look alive."

"I'm fine. Still in a whirl, but fine."

"You found their vehicles. You think they'll run?"

"We'd need tires, rubber hoses, batteries, and a tune up. I bet they'd run well. They haven't been used much."

"Good. The cattle are there?"

"Oh, yes. Lots of bulls. Big ones."

"We have a partner who wants to fatten them."

"They're wild. Haven't been handled, but they'll settle down."

"How will you tame them again?"

"Make yokes and hitch them. They'll settle down fast-hitched to another steer."

"Good. Thursday, we settle the sale up at his office."

"Good. It's a real buy."

"I doubt that anyone else would have tackled it. You have a mind for these kinds of deals."

"It sure isn't an office job." Excitement for the deal built fast, and he felt a lot like a whirling dervish. Spinning like crazy.

It must've shown, 'cause Sam laughed and held up a picture of him and Alma. "Is this your wife?"

"Yes."

"She like the place?"

"Loves it."

"Good. I can see it in her smile. I can't wait to go see this ranch of ours. You have help?"

"We left one fellow up there. Our guide. Long story. My man is hiring more today. He's also buying some more horses." How odd it felt, calling Jones "my man." Like a real ranch boss or something.

"They tell me they can get those bulldozers to somewhere close west of the ranch. I have some diesel tanks and an old pickup for you to use over there until we can get that other one running."

"Until they come with the Cat, we'll work on roundup."

"That sounds good. Have a seat. You can stay in town for a few nights, or you can take one of my cars back and forth to Lehi."

"I can drive back and forth, if you have a car I can use."

"Good. I may have a party at my house, and you can tell my friends all about the ranch."

"Whatever you want." Things were moving so fast he wasn't sure he could keep up. Influence Sam's friends? It would matter for what was coming. Hard to believe his life had gone into high gear like this all of a sudden.

"Would your girl like to attend it?"

"I don't know, but I can ask her." Would it matter to him if she was an Indian? He hoped not, 'cause that might cause some trouble between him and Sam.

"I didn't mean anything."

"I know, but Alma is well-spoken and a very sweet person. I'd be sure she has a suitable dress."

"Good. We don't need money invested in this ranch project, but I have others who might want to be partners in the next project we find."

Mark relaxed a bit. Sam was an expansive man. He simply wanted more profitable deals all the time. They went to lunch at the Mesa Country Club and he met some other men who were bankers and investors. They knew Sam had a project underway and that he would soon tell everyone his plans. But Sam kept it under wraps and they ate lunch in the glassed-in dining room looking off the hill at the Salt River Valley and the small town of Lehi.

After lunch, Sam took him by his large sprawling house and gave him the keys to his older Lincoln coupe.

"We'll meet at the office at eight." Sam left him to drive back to Jones's.

Back at the *jacal*, Mark spun the Lincoln to a skidding stop, kicking up debris. Alma ran out of her wall tent, stopped short beside the car. Ran her fingers over the dusty fender. Then she hurried to hug him when he climbed out.

Jones came over and admired it. "Fancy car."

"I'm simply borrowing it."

"I didn't figure you bought it to drive to the ranch," he laughed.

"It ain't high enough off the ground to make it. But our bulldozer is coming to build a road."

Jones shook his head. "Our bulldozer, huh? I ride horses, not tractors."

Amused, he laughed. "Have you found any help?"

"Two good boys that can ride and rope. They will help us. I told them we have to build corrals and such too, so they know what the job takes."

"Good. We'll see you later." He turned to her, hugging Alma's shoulder.

They went to their tent and she closed the flap when they were inside. The sun had warmed the structure. He held her, kissing her on the nose and then the lips. She began unbuttoning the blouse she wore, smiling at him as she did. He toed off his boots.

Later, he told her about Sam's plans. "He's having a party at his house when we close the deal. You're invited. We may have to buy you a dress."

She paused, looking up at him. "I don't have to go."

"Yes, you will. I'm not ashamed of you. In the future, you'll be my wife when she gets her divorce. I can afford to buy you a dress and you're not a tobacco store Indian maid. You dressed like the others in school."

She was silent for a moment. "When Jeff was killed, I went back to the reservation ways and dressed like a squaw. How you need me to dress for this party, I will do it. It will be different at the ranch when I work." She smiled, then laughed at his expression of mirth.

He hugged her. "You're a strong woman and I love you."

They slept in each other's arms until late afternoon.

Over the next few days, the ranch sale was closed. While Mark handled the business in Phoenix, Jones and the two new-hires took a pack train up to set up more of their needs.

He told her later about their day in the lawyer's office up in Mayer when they closed the buyout.

The HC Brand went with the ranch, as well, plus all the branded and un-branded animals in the vicinity of the deeded land. They would have the car, tractor, and truck titles, plus all the remaining furniture and horse tack, as well as water rights to the Verde River that Sam's lawyers found for them. When they were through making the sale, some cowboy cooked prime steaks out at the lawyer's ranch house and they celebrated.

"So, this is the man found that place for you?" Hall asked, more than a little full of good whiskey by this point.

"Yeah, Mark found it. And he's the man going to get it back in shape. Tell me who offered you more money after we made the deal."

"Neal Gipson. Lives up there. Wanted it for his boy. First, he tried to steal it. After he learned it had been sold, he offered more money. Tried to break the deal by raising the bid. He never wanted to give anything for it, but when he heard you'd bought it he had a walleyed fit."

Mark nodded. No surprise. He kept what he knew about the son to himself, though, hoping the kid didn't cause trouble.

"Well, we have work to do. We better get back to Phoenix. Thanks again." Mark shook Sam's hand.

Sam's man drove them back to Mesa. Mark parted and took the Lincoln back to Lehi. Jones had already gone back to the ranch with the two boys, Carlos and Byran Brown, so he didn't share their excitement, but they had a big time.

"The deed lists me as part-owner of the ranch." Mark whooped and swung Alma around as they danced in the yard. She was as high as he was and had had nothing to drink. The next day, they went back to the ranch on horse-back, so they missed Sam's party. While she was willing to go, she was also relieved. They were returning to the ranch again and he could hardly contain his excitement.

The cattle business proved wild and Western. He used clamps—a large wood-en handled steel tool—on the bulls. The clamps bloodlessly cut off the hormones to their body and their masculinity, something Mark learned in FFA in high school. But bulls had to be fore-footed or in a squeeze chute to do it. They roped, branded them, and clamped off their balls. It wasn't easy work—most of the stag bulls were over twelve hundred pounds. They only found a few aged purebred bulls left alive that Hancock had bought years earlier. They left them, though Sam was looking for new ones to replace the inbreeding going on in the cowherd.

———

THE DAY WAS SET UP for the dozers to arrive. Mark had ridden over to the Bumble Bee side the day before to meet them. It proved to be cold with light snow, so Alma stayed home. He used a tent and had lots of bedding on his packhorse. The dozer didn't get there until late afternoon and the driver, Frank Roe, started the dozer he brought with the starter engine. He wasn't bringing the other over until the following week. It was fine with Mark. Frank could unload that one by himself. Mark had a road to clear. Once un-loaded, he cleared off a place with the dozer for the man to turn his truck and trailer around. He offered him supper, but the driver was anxious to get back home that night.

Mark ran the dozer for a few hours, clearing a dry wash crossing and start-ing up the next mountain portion that was so washed out. He slept the night in his tent. At dawn, he made coffee, ate tortillas wrapped around cold beans and bacon that Alma had sent along, and worked another day on the road. With the clack of the tracks and him working the cable lifting the blade up and down with a lever over his head, the job went slow and the Cat used a fifty-gallon barrel of diesel fuel a day. Jones and Alma rode over on horseback to see how it was go-ing. He told them in less than a week he'd be at the house at his current progress.

She stayed with him and Jones took the horses back. They moved the camp closer to the end of the road. Two days later, they made it to the ranch and the road was smooth enough to drive over. Mark and Alma drove to Prescott to call Sam and tell him he could drive up. They took some barrels along in the old pickup to carry fuel in.

Mark called from a phone at the oil supply company. "You can drive up, but don't expect conveniences. We don't have indoor toilets, lights, or running water."

Sam laughed and promised to be there. The two of them went back to the ranch, and they took a bath in a galvanized tub to get rid of the diesel smell that had saturated them.

"I'm glad you can stand me smelling like a gallon of diesel." He shaved in a smoky mirror and she bathed in the same water she had scrubbed him in earlier—with some more hot water added.

"I didn't smell much better, so I couldn't tell."

"I guess you better get ready to meet Sam. He'll be up here tomorrow."

"I'll wear a skirt and blouse."

"Good. Not that I am upset, but I want you to fit in my world."

"I won't lose you by being a squaw."

"Oh, my." He glanced back and smiled.

———

CALEB DROVE SAM OUT. THEY arrived in his late-model Lincoln, covered with a layer of thick dust from the road. Sam crawled out wearing an overcoat and beat his britches leg with a snap-brim hat. "Nice job on the road," he said to Mark, turning to face Alma. "This must be Alma."

"Yes, I am. I am glad to meet you, sir."

Mark beamed.

"You people are real pioneers." Sam shook his head, swinging around to see the mountains that hemmed it in. "Can we start hauling out cattle?"

"We can finish the loading chute, and I guess taking cattle out with bob trucks will work. I'd like you to use my friend Noah Gaines for some of it. He saved my life on a hauling deal."

"I'll do that. I know and like him. Late Evans down at Chandler is set up to sort them. He wants to feed the thin ones. Late is a good cattle trader. I've talked with him about his part and he explained how he'd divide them. He would sell the cull cows and broken-down bulls to a butcher who uses them in lunchmeat. The younger ones will be fed and sent to packers. The market for beef is good."

"My friend, Noah Grimes, who hauled the horses for us, is in consideration?"

"Yes, Grimes even bought another truck and he's our trucker. Let's start shipping next week. Evans can split them up down there. Can he haul two dozen head per truck?"

"Maybe less of those big bulls." Mark held the front door open for him.

Sam nodded and stepped inside, looking around at the progress they'd made on the house. "Looks good in here. You've done a good job." He glanced from Alma back to Mark. "I'm concerned about the young calves that need to be weaned."

"Do you have pasture down there for them?"

"Evans mentioned a man down by Tucson who would take them on shares."

He and Sam took seats on the wooden kitchen chairs.

Alma brought them coffee. "I'm sorry. I have only canned milk, no cream."

"Alma, it sure won't matter to me." Sam smiled. "I know this isn't New York City, but you're making yourselves a fine place here."

Caught up in the excitement, they all laughed.

"I think we should haul off all the older cattle we can and get them off this range," Mark said. "They eat the most, and if we can get three runs a week out of here, we'd dent them fast. I don't know if the boys and I can even round them up that fast. But we can tell the truckers when we will have more cattle. We also need them to bring up some baled hay to feed our horses and cattle that are held in the pens."

"I'll have them haul it in next week when they come for the first loads. Did you hear anything out of the Gipsons?"

"No, but I'll tell you about that son." Mark explained about him shooting at Jones and having that bridle on his horse.

"You did the right thing. He better count his lucky stars you didn't shoot him."

"I'm trying to get over killing people." Mark stood when Jones came in the room. "This man is Dirty Shirt Jones, my foreman. This is Sam."

"How are you?" Jones put out his hand. "You fly in?"

They all laughed, and Alma brought him coffee.

"Well, Mister Jones, how do you like things up here?"

"Fine, but you just call me Jones. There is too much work up here and if it wasn't on horseback, I wouldn't stay here."

Sam laughed aloud. "Nothing like getting things straight at the start."

The plan was to haul out all the old cows and bulls first. By law, they had to be branded to transport them and also brand inspected. They planned to do that at Evan's Chandler ranch with a permit from the state brand inspector's office, since it was so far out to the ranch for their man to travel up there each time. Things went smoothly.

———

MARK RE-GRADED THE ROAD IN two days and they were ready for the trucks by following Wednesday. When Noah stepped down out of his rig that first morning, he shook Mark's hand.

"I sure appreciate you getting me this business, Mark. Guess we'll be busy."

"Hey, when you came and got us at Fort McDowell, we were stranded. You saved our lives."

"I was glad to help you out, pardner." He glanced around. "Looks like we got two loads ready today. They're pretty spooky."

"Sure are, but the corrals are fortified and should hold them."

Noah's father, Frank, drove the second truck and did lots of gazing around, amazed at the ranch having been empty for so long.

After everyone stacked off the hay, the two trucks were loaded and headed out for Chandler. Mark told Noah they'd have two more loads in the pens no later than Friday.

Things were set.

Even Alma rode with the crew to round up the next shipment. The cattle were spooky and some ran off, but they had enough at the pens each drive to cut off the cows and calves they planned to keep, then brand them and their calves for release. With close to two days in the saddle, they'd branded over a hundred head and things were moving quickly. Noah and Frank hauled off fifty more head of bawling cattle and they went back to work.

Mark had a logbook and a stub of pencil to make entries for the cows turned out with calves. He was on a high each day when they rode out to get more. In three weeks, they'd sent four hundred and fifty head to town. He planned to slow things. The big cattle remaining hid out when they came looking for them. The easy part was done.

He sent word by Noah that they needed a ten-day break. He took everyone to Prescott in the old International truck Sam had brought up for them and treated them to a steak dinner. The two cowboys wrapped up in blankets and rode in the back—those boys didn't mind a thing about that. They were ready to see the bright lights.

They bought supplies and found a man who had two stock dogs. He sold them for thirty dollars and guaranteed them to be heelers. They'd need them to catch the wild ones. Dressed up in heavy clothes, he hugged Alma and kissed her. They admired the Christmas lights in the stores and began to get in the spirit of the season.

"A year ago, I was in France freezing my ass off on the front lines. Today I'm freezing my ass off in Preskit and happy as a lark to have you. How lucky can a soldier get in twelve months?"

"It is all like a wonderful dream," Alma said. "I was so sad when the news came about Jeff. I went to hide on the reservation. I never expected you to come along, seduce me, and have it all turn out so good."

"It is just the start. We are partners in a ranch and we have shipped close to fifty thousand dollars' worth of cattle to market, by my calculations. And we still have more."

"Oh, Mark, I am so happy. This is the best Christmas in my life."

They went home and honeymooned some more. The days ran into the New Year. They had two loads of cattle at the pens when Noah arrived on the first Tuesday of the new year. The big man, dressed in a Scotch plaid coat and knit cap against the brisk north wind, looked concerned.

"How are you?"

"I'm fine. Alma's relative sent me word to tell her that her grandmother is not doing well and wishes to see her."

"I'll go get her and you can tell her."

"If she needs to go, I'll take her and bring her back later."

"That's mighty good of you."

Noah put his arm on Mark's shoulder. "My business has doubled. Not only you and Sam, but other folks have found me, too. I know it was doing this that did it. I'm getting more cattle and things to haul. It is really good, since I have two trucks to pay for, and Dad loves it."

Alma joined them, and Mark told her the message and Noah's offer.

"I will go get ready. She is a very important person in my life."

"Go," Mark said. "You need me to come down, send word and I'll be there."

"I will go pack." She looked a little downfallen about the news. "I won't be gone long," she promised as they walked back to the house.

"Take as much time as you need." He waved her on. Lord, as much as she had done for him, she didn't need to apologize about going away for her family. There had been references made to him about how her grandmother made her attend school even when she didn't want to go.

Alma left to ride into town with Noah, promising to be back in a few days. They had a hard time parting in the warmer-than-normal sunshine. Once he'd seen her off, he and the crew rode off with their young dogs to round up more cattle.

The weather remained warmer than usual for January. They found fifteen mature bulls in the brush, and between the dogs and hard riding, delivered them to the corrals at the headquarters.

"We're getting better at this," Jones teased as they unsaddled their horses. The angry bulls fought each other and bawled in the pens.

"There's a car coming," Carlos said with his ear turned to the west.

Jones frowned. "Who in the hell's coming here?"

Something was wrong. Mark's belly turned sour. Whose car was it?

It was Sam's Lincoln. He set out to greet him, feeling weak-kneed. Why? What in the hell was wrong? Why did he feel so struck by something fatal?

"Mark, we need to go to the house and talk," Sam said, getting out.

"What's wrong? What's happened? Is Alma all right?"

Sam stopped, dropped his chin, and took hold of his arm. "A drunk ran her over on the Lehi Road in the wagon. Mark, she died before the ambulance got there. I'm sorry. You've had enough hell in your life."

He squeezed his eyes shut. This was a bad dream. Incoming artillery boomed, the machine guns rattled incisively, the copper scent of the dead filled his nostrils. Mark turned, staggering off on rubber legs to a little hill behind the ranch house where he fell to his knees sobbing. Oh Lord, why her? She was an angel. No—not his beautiful, sweet, little Alma. Not her. He wanted to kill someone. Anyone would do.

8

JONES WORE A NEW WHITE shirt. The two cowboys, hats in hand, stood in fresh clothing beside him. Several of Alma's relatives clustered around Mark. They had spoken to him and squeezed his hands. Her aunt stepped forward and kissed him, thanking him for what he did by lifting her from her sorrows. But no one was going to lift him from his own losses. He never knew until today what people meant when they said they were heart-broken. His heart was shattered into tiny pieces—the heart that loved her, kept her happy and safe, promised to cherish her.

And he was afraid he'd never put the pieces together again.

The preacher spoke some in Pima, some in English. She looked good in her native dress, like he had found her in the pony parking lot. Wrapped in a new trade blanket of red, blue, and green stripes, it suited her more than the finest dress. He prayed God took her hand and told her how he would miss not having her. After a long silence, everyone looked down as if praying with him. They rode in the funeral home's car to the reservation cemetery. The outline of the McDowell Mountains in the north looked blue-purple in the distance.

In his mind's eye, he saw her and him chasing horses, her turning his way and laughing with sunlight on her blue-black hair. They disappeared into the skirts of mist around Four Points. Snow on the peaks gleamed against the azure sky. He swallowed hard. She was gone.

He was surprised to see his father and stepmother and walked over to talk to them. "Where is the new baby?" His voice didn't sound like him.

"He's at her mother's. Sam sent us word. I'd heard you lived with an Indian woman. We were sorry to hear what happened. Sam told me you and him are partners in a big ranch."

"Yes, it's up in Bloody Basin. We've been working cattle. It was a mess."

"Folks have been talking around Chandler about all the cattle you've shipped."

Mark nodded. It was good to talk about everyday things for that moment. "I get time one day, I'll drop by and see you and the new one. Excuse me for now, though. I need to speak to Alma's folks before they leave."

When he hugged his stepmother, she whispered, "God be with you. I will burn a candle for you in my church."

"Thanks." Tears burned at his eyes, but he shoved them away. Why did she have to go and leave him?

He trudged over to talk to her family. "How is her grandmother?"

A small woman with a dried-up apple face waddled forward and held up her arms for him. "God bless you my son. You made her days bright after her loss."

"Thank you, Grandmother, and all of you. I was so pleased to have shared the short time I had with her...."

He could say no more, and Sam took him to the car, holding his arm.

"Where do you want to go?"

"Back to the ranch. Do I still have a job?"

"Hell, yes. What do you need?"

"Another load of hay. We still have the wild ones to catch and we'll start cutting off calves and cull old cows to ship."

"You want to take some time off or anything? Jones can run the ranch."

"I'll best be able to get over her working as any other way. I love the ranch. And she's with me there."

"Fine. I'll let Caleb drive the boys back up and I'll take you."

"Sam, just take me to Lehi. I'll drive your old coupe up there and use it. You don't need to go clear up there."

"Son, I can't believe we fell into this ranch deal. I know right now your loss of her is tough. But you and those three Indians have done so much. Well, I can't hardly believe we've come this far already."

He shook hands with Sam, then climbed in the older car, started it, and honked to signal at Sam. Out the car window were bare stalks of the past year's cotton. Would there ever be another woman in his life to fill the empty gap in his heart? He beat the boys back to the ranch and was about in bed when they stomped past the house. They went on up to the bunkhouse, laughing and joking, their feet clomping on the hard earth. Alone in the bed under the covers, he stared at the dark underside of the shakes. The months ahead would be hard, but he'd make it—he had a ranch. Alma had loved it, too.

———

IN LATE JANUARY, SAM THREW a party at his house and sent word for Mark to come down to attend it. He had a room in the San Jose Motel in Mesa. In it, he found a new Western-cut black suit, starched white shirts, a Zuni bolo tie, and a new pair of black Justin boots, as well as two pairs of tan riders, and some snap shirts with a hand carved belt and an Indian-made silver buckle. To top it off, there was a snowy 40X Stetson hat. He sure had gone shopping for the first time in ages.

Sam's note to him said, *Be at the house before five and greet my friends for me. I will be late.*

He was there by four-thirty. Sam's housekeeper, Anna, told him the boss expected him to be the host, since he had business to handle. Mark walked around the spacious house and studied the Western art Sam had collected. In the den was the large painting of the sexy woman in the cloud scene used as an ad for A-1 Beer. When the doorbell rang, he answered it and a tall blonde woman in dark nylon stockings came into the tiled alcove. He guessed her to be in her mid-twenties. When he took her fur coat, she had quite a figure with her cleavage exposed and a diamond necklace that must have cost thousands hung over the sight.

"Linda Acosta." A hand held out. Her voice was musical.

"Mark Shaw."

"Oh, you're Sam's ranching partner?"

"Yes, ma'am. Can I get you a drink? We're the first ones here."

"What do you have?"

"To tell you the truth, I don't know, but we can go find out. Anna said there's a bartender here somewhere."

She took his arm and they went back in the house and found Arnold, who made her a dry martini with an olive in it. He escorted her into the spacious living room.

They took seats apart on the couch and she answered questions, remarking that she was in Arizona to make a movie.

"You're a movie star? I'm sorry. I've been overseas in the army, came back and worked this ranch in Bloody Basin. I don't know a thing about the arts or the movie business."

"This is my fourth film and I'm in big letters on the screen in this one. I want to do a Western, and Sam says your ranch is the place to film it. He says that real Indians work for you and they could be in the movie."

Mark smiled. He wasn't going to tell her it was just another old run-down ranch. Her perfume even smelled expensive. There was a lot of woman squeezed in that dress. Sam always had a deal going to make more money— now movies. His mind skittered from one thing to another, the woman made him so nervous.

The conversation got around to where he was staying. "San Jose Motel on west Main Street. Sam's got me covered. Nice partner."

"Did you buy this suit at Porters Western Store?" She fingered the material.

"My partner chose this one." His flesh rippled from her touch.

"Very nice suit."

"Thanks. I usually wear Levi's."

She laughed, deep throated and sexy. Arnold showed up with another dry martini and she traded him glasses. "You are a darling, sir."

When he left, she quietly asked, "Are you a Mormon?"

"Lord, no ma'am. I simply don't drink alcohol."

"I admire you. They tell me you have medals from the war."

"Some. I've been trying to shed that part of my life."

"I can understand."

No way in hell, but she was nice to say so.

People started to show up and she went along to help him greet them. They hung up fur coats and men's top coats and directed them to go and feast. During a break they had in the incoming guests, he said, "I'm ruining your evening. I can do this."

"No. I find you flattering and I enjoy your company. You're a very unpretentious man and I like that."

"You still don't have much. I'm just a cowboy." He opened the door to a rangy suntanned man with a crop of white hair. "Good evening. Welcome to Sam's place. There's finger food in the room to the left and Arnold can fix your drinks."

"Thank you. My name's Larkin. I take it you're Mark Shaw. I have a large feedlot. Sam ever makes you mad, come and see me."

"Thanks."

His gray-haired wife, dripping in diamond jewelry, took his arm. "Carl, this is that actress I told you about. Linda Acosta."

"How nice to meet you, young lady. My wife has told me all about your career."

"Thank you, sir," she said, a little too nice.

When Larkin and his wife left them, Mark turned to Linda. "You knew him."

She made a scowl. "Without her, he is much too handy."

He was amused. "I guess that goes with the job."

"No, it does not. But some men don't understand."

Sam finally arrived, kissed her on the cheek, and thanked her. "You two have done a wonderful job here. Now come in and join the party."

Mark gave him a sharp look. Damn the man. This meeting of his with Miss Movie Star was all Sam's work. She hung back, and Sam went on to greet everyone out in the big room.

She stepped in and took his arm. "I asked Sam for the job. I wanted to meet you. You're a pretty level guy. I live in a world of phony people who think they are someone and aren't. Do you dance?"

"I once did."

"Good. Try and spoil the girl from California."

"Yes ma'am."

They danced, and she acted impressed. She drank some more dry ones, and then they danced more 'til supper. Seated side by side, they went through the courses. She leaned over and whispered, "Is your bed in the motel a double one?"

Struck speechless, he couldn't think of a reply. It hadn't been long since he lost Alma, but it was hard not to be tempted by this lovely movie star.

"I'm sorry...." He didn't know what to say.

The man next to him held a platter of baked potatoes out to him. Glad for the interruption, he took one and passed them on. One of the waiters delivered Linda a well-done filet and him a medium-rare steak that filled his dinner plate.

Her eyes flew open. "You must love beef."

"I do. And I grow them."

Linda did everything she could to lure him away to his room and bed. She had no shame. He was tempted. Any man would be, but all he could think was how would Alma feel? She wouldn't want him to be alone, but it was too soon. Besides. A movie star? He had visions of her up on the ranch hunting for a shower. He had no wish for her style of living. It would only be a fling and that was wrong. Just wrong. When he did look for another woman, it would be for a life together. Not some cheap roll in the hay.

At the end of the evening, with everyone streaming out the doors except those who would spend the night, he told her one last time that he was sorry.

Linda regarded him with sultry eyes. "No need to be. I know you must really miss your wife. I wish we could be more than friends, but I have a career to build and you have a ranch. It's best."

She kissed him on the cheek. "Good luck cowboy. Maybe some other time, some other place."

It was like being in a movie. He couldn't help smiling and playing his part. "See you in the movies, darlin'."

She laughed, trailing her painted fingernails along his jaw, swung into her coat, and left.

Mark felt good about the whole thing—better than going home feeling guilty over something he shouldn't've done. She really was a nice woman. He'd watch for her on the movie screen.

He stayed to help Sam clean up. His partner seemed a bit surly. Mark wouldn't be surprised if the man hadn't tried to set him up with Linda.

Better luck next time, partner.

———

LATER AT SAM'S OFFICE, HE sat in the leather chair while Sam talked on the phone to someone about a deal. The man really enjoyed doing business. He hung up and looked at Mark.

"Hey, sorry things didn't work out with Linda, there, cowboy. She's almost too much for me, too."

"Yes, she's a big deal. I'm just not ready yet—though I'll admit I was tempted."

With a wide grin, Sam leaned back in his swivel chair and tented his fingers over his chest. "Can't blame you there, but I do understand." He slapped a hand down on his desk. "So, back to business. How many more head of cattle do we have to sell?"

"Well, Jones and I think about two-fifty, plus the calf crop. I'll keep about a hundred heifers, if you want to build a herd, grow them out this winter, and bring them back next spring. There were way too many cattle up there and the range needs some rest."

"I can understand that. Now, Late Evans wants you to look at some bulls for next year. They're Domino stock."

"We need some fresh blood, and that should give us a start on a real herd. I want to clear the alfalfa field and re-sow it. There will be some ditch repair and seed plus fuel expenses, but eighty acres of alfalfa would be a great asset to that place."

"That's fine with me. Hire some carpenters and fix the house. If we ever want to sell it in the future, it will be the first thing they'll look at. Plus, you'll need to entertain some of my prospective associates. People like that cowboy atmosphere, with steaks cooking on the fire. Would you mind them making a movie out there? They'll leave us with a set we can rent to other movie makers."

"Sounds like fun."

"Good. You'll need about a half dozen nice bedrooms added to the current residence. Plumb them, and in time we'll have electricity out there."

"Take a lot of poles and wire."

"Tell Jones and the men thanks, I know they've worked hard. I'll either drive up there or you can drive down in two weeks. We have sold close to sixty thousand dollars in cattle. Do those boys need some money?"

"They'd probably like some. We put on a new hand, Jim, the fella you sent to guide us up there last month."

"Good. I know you can use him. I'll have Hazel make you a checkbook. Be sure to legibly write on the stub where it went and who you paid. You've done well. When you come in, drop it off and she can get the details and you can take it back with you."

"So, movie people are coming?"

"Get the house done. I'll tell them to bring their own tent for now."

With business over, he drove to Chandler to see his new half-brothers and sister. It was one of those rare, beautiful winter days, when the sun shines down out of a brilliant blue sky and no wind comes off the snowcapped mountains to chill the flesh. When he drove in, his dad was busy overhauling a John Deere tractor. He came over in his shirt sleeves, wiping greasy hands on a rag. Lenore came to the doorway in an apron and waved. Sam had given Mark two hundred dollars in cash and he bought some hard candy for the children when he filled up the coupe.

Dang, he should'a brought them more gifts or something. He passed the sweets around, so each got a handful and they went off screeching, chasing each other. The baby slept through it all in her crib in the living room. He stood, looking down at her for a long while, imagining another life.

Never mind that. Lenore gave him a hug and thanked him. He kissed her cheek. Family was a pretty good thing to have. They sat in the living room on the hand-me-down sofa and he told them about the ranch. Their house was clean as one got a shack. But it made him recall the days growing up, them living in sharecropper outfits and going up to Congress to his grandfather's ranch.

She perked coffee on a butane stove, and they drank at a wooden table like the one they had back then while the kids played in the other room. She did have a noisy Kelvinator fridge that ran on gas. A light bulb hung down in each room. Country living.

The baby stirred in her crib. He rose. "Okay if I hold her?"

Lenore nodded, and he gathered her into his arms and rocked the warm wiggly baby while they talked about rounding up the cattle and the success he'd had on the ranch.

"I cleared a road into the place with a cable blade Cat. See, Dad? All those things you taught me came to good use."

"May I ask you something?" Lenore asked cautiously.

"Sure, what's that?"

"Do you still hear the war?"

"Sometimes." He leaned down to kiss the child's cheek. "More now that Alma's gone. Especially at night."

Her eyes darkened, but she nodded like that was all she wanted to know.

Before he left, he paid his dad for the saddle and put it in the trunk. "I need to go home."

They shook hands and Dad patted his shoulder.

"Son, I was worried. You talking about horses and riding off to get lost. But my Lord, you've done well for yourself. Thanks for coming by." Then he handed his wife the saddle money.

They must be living close. He'd have thought the old man would've spent that on himself or her—not put it in the bread fund. He'd have to help them in some way. He drove off, leaving a wake of dust and headed for a lonely night.

When he reached the Tucson highway, he stopped.

No one was going to take Alma's place. He'd found that out the night before when offered a night in bed with a sensational movie star. Maybe he needed a trip to Nogales across the border, where he'd pay for what he got, with no holds barred. No ties or guilt trips.

He turned the steering wheel south. Since it was Sam's car, he left it on the American side at dusk and took a wreck of a taxi to Canal Street. The cab man asked for fifty cents. He paid him.

The streets were noisy with life. Laughing, singing, women strutting. Mexican trumpet music came through the open doors of the cantinas. A drunk staggered onto the boardwalk, letting out clouds of smoke and the stench of beer and old spittoons. He bumped Mark's shoulder, glanced at him with rheumy eyes.

"Sorry." Mark pushed away and went on down the street, past blowsy women leaning against the fronts of one saloon after another.

Was this truly what he wanted? None would compare to his beautiful Alma. A man could do better than this, surely.

He turned a corner and walked on. Ahead was a fountain where a lovely young woman sat, dangling bare feet in the water. The sun was setting, sending a golden hue over the adobe *haciendas*. Her black hair rose around her in a puff of wind, then settled on her shoulders like a silken scarf. As he drew closer, she glanced up and smiled, looking for an instant so much like Alma his stomach clenched.

He nodded. *"Buenos tardes."*

Her wide grin made him glad he remembered the correct greeting for early evening. She returned the salutation and added, "Sit if you like."

Her English was better than his Spanish.

He sat, leaving a wide space between them. Spray from the fountain glistened in her hair.

"You came down from the United States?"

He studied her, tried to guess her age, then wondered why. "Yes."

"Why did you come? For a *puta?*"

Heat crawled up his neck and flushed his face. "No. I—yes, I guess. But I've changed my mind."

She kicked at the water, laughed. "Take me to the *cantina* where we will dance, and we can maybe change your mind back."

"I will take you to dance because I'm lonely and you're not a *puta*. Are you?"

Her own face reddening, she shook her head. "No. I am not but I am lonely, too." She slid off the rock wall of the fountain, stuck her feet into a pair of leather *huraches,* and turned in a circle. "Am I not pretty enough to dance with an American?"

He held out his hand, took her small brown fingers in his grip. "Oh, yes. You are pretty enough. Only to dance, though."

She steered him through backstreets away from the touristy area to a small *cantina* where a young man sat on a stool, playing music on a box guitar. He sang in a pure tenor voice about the love of his life leaving him for another. Couples danced slowly, the girls' brightly colored skirts swirling with each turn. The place smelled of candles and herbs and beautiful women. *Sombreros* and fans of all colors decorated the walls. The floor was hard-stomped clay.

They found a table in a dark corner and ordered drinks. He stood.

"Dance with me?"

The singer went directly into another song, this one of a happier time when love did not betray lovers.

Mark held her loosely and they found the rhythm together. Here he was, dancing again. First with Linda and now this pretty girl. He hadn't danced in ages, since the long-ago days at the USO, but he'd been fair to good at it once. Linda approved. This girl was better, and he went with her movements. Soon she snuggled closer, the top of her head under his chin so that her hair tickled.

The music stopped too soon, and the singer rose, laying his guitar on the stool. He spoke in Spanish, something about taking a break but coming back. Mark needed to learn better Spanish.

She led him back to their table. "He will be right back if you wish to stay and dance with me some more." She tilted her head up and grinned with mischief. "I promise not to ask you to take me in the back. I just wish to dance the night away and forget my sadness."

He held her chair, then sat down across from her so he could see her face when she smiled. "That is all I wish to do too. Forget sadness."

So that's what they did. She told him her sad story and he told her his. And they danced some more. He held her close with no fear of what might happen.

"You know, the night is almost over, and I don't even know your name."

"Nor I yours. Let it stay that way, for both of us." She gazed up at him.

He thought about that for a while, then nodded in agreement.

Cocks were crowing down the street when the *cantina* closed, and he offered to walk her home. She took his hand, kissing the fingertips. "No need, *gentil hombre*. I am just a ways down the street. You will go home tonight?"

"Yes, lovely lady." He watched her till she turned into a small gate with vines growing on it, then he walked into the tourist section where he found a ride back across the border to the Lincoln. In his mind, he would always think of her as Dolores.

———

THAT SPRING, THE MOVIE BUSINESS became a reality. They arrived wearing pith helmets and shorts. He cleared them a site down on the Verde and they moaned and groaned about the wilderness and no phones, claiming that the merchants nearby were robbing them on material prices. But it was just part of the post war days of building material shortages. There had not been any business during the war, so the recovering industry was strapped for suppliers. He'd learned that himself remodeling and expanding the ranch house. He finally found them a lumber company in Prescott that made them a good supplier.

Sam thought Mark could do miracles with what he did hiring local labor and ending up with things as nice as he had. Rosita became his housekeeper, cook, and general supervisor of the ranch when he was gone. She would read the crew the tasks he wanted done when he was in Phoenix or away. A short Mexican war widow in her forties, she ran things well, whether he was there or not.

He planted over forty acres of the large flat land and his new alfalfa drew every deer in Arizona to the field. Each morning and night, his men cleared them out with the noisy shotguns, and they hunted some for meat. The crop prospered and by midsummer they cut and stacked hay. It was a good plan and they made do with the small Ford. Over near Camp Verde, he bought an International with a cable frontend loader and a beaver board. The rest of the cuttings were stacked by the tractor. A team pulled the load delivered on the front end, and then they dragged it up to the top of the board with horses driven by Jones. The haystacks soon were piled high.

His crew beamed over their accomplishments, and so did Mark. In between cuttings, they overhauled the International tractor, got the truck running, and the car, too. But Mark still drove the Lincoln coupe.

Sometimes he thought of the pretty *senorita* in Nogales, and the evening they'd shared, but he never went back.

When Linda came to star in the movie, he took her on rides over the ranch and she fell in love with Red. Still, he made it clear that friendship was all he wanted. It wasn't long before they actually enjoyed each other's company without any complications.

He found the movie making bit boring. They shot every scene over and over again. Sam rented them ranch horses and furnished a power plant on a flatbed truck, all for a fee. Plus, they paid rent to use the ranch itself. Mark chuckled at Sam's ability to make money, and the money was indeed great in the two months they were there. His three-man crew was paid a hundred dollars a day for working in the film. All of the boys bought new saddles made in Prescott and could not believe the money they earned.

Carlos told him they were going to have a rodeo at Camp Verde and asked him to come along. He let them drive the refurbished Buick, but told them not to drive it if they were drinking or he'd fire them. He agreed to meet them there and told Linda he'd pick her up.

How long had it been since he rode a bronc in competition? Six months before the war? Maybe that long ago, but he might try again.

Linda was excited as they drove down to Camp Verde. He got entered in the bronc riding. A friend offered to let him use his bareback rigging, and another guy loaned him his dogging horse and said he'd haze for twenty-five percent of what he won. Mark didn't care. He'd not win anything anyway, and he'd pay the guy ten bucks for his troubles.

Jones was with him, telling him how this horse he'd drawn would buck. Linda was holding up a long-tailed dress and trying to keep up with them as they headed for the chute. Someone must've recognized her and told the rodeo announcer.

With borrowed spurs, gloves, and rigging, they helped him get ready to ride.

Wilcox, the announcer, told the crowd this next horse was a man killer. The best bucking horse in Arizona. Killer Bear. Mark looked up and frowned at the man, then turned back to the horse under him and tried to recall those days back when he rode.

Jones was talking in his ear more than that rascal ever talked in one day.

"Ladies and gentlemen, we have a lady on the gate looking worried about the next rider, Mark Shaw. He brought along the leading lady in the movie being shot on Shaw's ranch, the HC. Let's welcome Linda Lacosta!"

The applause from the crowd readied Mark for what was coming, and they turned Killer Bear out the gate. His spurs connected good with the horse's shoulders, way down underneath him. Then, as if on springs, Bear soared high in the air and dropped down in a backbone-jarring landing. Bear kicked over his rear and went plunging away. Laid back on the horse, spurring him hard from down to up, the crowd went wild. He must've made the eight-second whistle, but he never heard it. The pickup men came charging in, telling him to get off.

His hand out of the rigging, he slipped over on the back of the pickup man's saddle. Once on the ground, he took his hat off, waved at the crowd, and headed for the chutes. Linda appeared from behind a gate into the arena. He swept her up in his arms, held her high, baring her gorgeous legs, pretty as Marilyn Monroe's. The flash photo by the publicity man made the cover of *Life* magazine the next week and Sam had one framed for each of them.

He scored an 82 and won the bronc riding. Thirty minutes later, he downed a steer in eleven flat and won the bulldogging. He always said Camp Verde Rodeo spoiled him so bad, he had to rodeo.

His only other date he ever had with Linda was when the studio paid his way to Hollywood for the premier showing of *Under Arizona Skies*. They suited him in a tux and a new 100X beaver he got to keep. He never felt more like a poodle dog on a leash than he did for all that.

9

FTER THAT, HE DIDN'T HEAR from Linda much, except for an occasional letter that smelled of lavender and told him about this or that famous male star escorting her somewhere. She hoped to make him envious, but he was happy for her and glad he'd made the decision he had about staying on the ranch. Oh, he met rodeo buckle bunnies and widow women with big ranches looking for a man for their bed. He never paid them any mind.

The ranch looked perfect—its fame as a movie site, the large-bodied Hereford herd, the green eighty acres of alfalfa. The ranch house was equipped with the war surplus generator he seldom used and running water designed to run on gravity with lots of pressure at the house and corrals.

Sam came up in his new 1954 Lincoln four-door and they had a sit down. A rich man wanted their ranch and was willing to pay one-and-a-half million dollars for it.

Sam leaned back in the wooden chair at the table. "That's six hundred thousand dollars to you. Plus, I've got a hundred and sixty acres down in Paradise Valley I'll give you to have your own place down there. Are you interested? This offer is so wild I could not believe it, Mark. We've had fun building this place, but that's three times its value." He shook his head. "I won't sell it unless you agree. But you can live like you want and do what you want when we sell it. I know, I know—you have sweet memories riding up here with pack horses and you've never really gotten over sweet Alma. I am sorry about that, but you have contacts in the movies, you rodeo, you stock contract, and you can do what you want the rest of your life on this much money."

Close to speechless, he sat with his eyes closed. Who would pay that much for this land with nothing fancy on it? A fool, no doubt.

"I need to talk to Jones. He helped me the most. I'll talk to him tomorrow." It was enough to blow a fella's mind, that much money, but they had worked damned hard and he liked the idea of the ranch Sam was offering in addition to the money. He needed to live and own a ranch, not live in one of those beehives in the city.

"Fine. I know. But we can't hardly pass this offer up."

"I'm sure he'll go along. Let us talk. The ranch deal sells it for me."

Sam agreed with him and they both went off to bed.

Mark hardly slept that night for imagining what he could do with that much money. It was more than he'd ever dreamed of. At breakfast, he told Jones they needed to check things on horseback.

Jones frowned. "Isn't Sam here? You going to leave him alone here?"

"Yep. Come on. We need to talk."

Jones shrugged off whatever and ate his cereal.

They rode up to Robber's Roost, a false front city where the studio tried to make the actor Cliff Edwards a star like Roy and Gene. It didn't work. Mark had earned three hundred dollars for an eight-second bronc ride as a stunt man dressed like Edwards. Convinced him he didn't want to be a movie star. Not that anyone had asked him.

When he and Jones dismounted and sat on the boardwalk in front of the Red Dog Saloon, Jones threw small rocks out in the street. The wind stirred dust devils and smelled of pine wood.

"What do you want out of our partnership?" Mark wiped sweat away with his bandana.

He shrugged. "Nothing. I have had a good time up here. Is it over?"

"Is there a farm in Lehi you'd like to have?"

"As a matter of fact, I was down there a few weeks ago and there's a farm at the foot of the hill. Forty acres of alfalfa, good water rights. They wanted twelve thousand dollars for it."

"I'll buy it for you."

Jones blinked at him in disbelief. "How did you get so gawdamn rich? You can fire me. I won't be mad."

"You recall that stud horse you sold before you asked me?"

"That was a long time ago. We were broke."

"Well, Sam's selling the ranch. It is for lots of money and he wants us happy. He knows we built this place and made him a boatload of cash doing it. People said he was greedy. He never cheated me out of a nickel. But the price for this ranch would have bought Phoenix when I went in the service, and folks would have said he paid too much." Mark stood, brushed off the seat of his pants. "Let's go. He's anxious to go back. I'm sure we'll need to show this new man the ranch and how it works."

Jones nodded, looking all confused—like he'd went cross-eyed or something.

"Tomorrow I'll go buy your new place." Mark patted him on the shoulder. "Don't you go passing out on me or anything."

Jones grinned like a possum. "You know there are things in my people's lore about a horse leading a man to riches. I think Red did that for us."

"Yes, he led you, Alma, and me here. You knew that day we buried her. I wanted to have her buried up here, but you said no. Sure pleased I didn't. I can go and leave flowers anytime when I get to missing her." And miss her he did. But it had been a long time, and plenty of water was under the bridge.

Jones nodded. Obviously, he knew the pain, but one thing was for sure. There would be more pain for both of them to leave this ranch. The memory of her still was inside his brain. She rode these hills and he couldn't ever stop seeing her that way. Hard to figure if it would ever fade. Better though than the guns he no longer heard.

The day dawned sunny and soon turned hot and dusty. That didn't matter much. It could've been raining lizards and cactus, wouldn't have stopped the ranch inspection by the buyer from going through. A long black Cadillac arrived first thing while Mark and Jones were drinking their second cup of coffee on the verandah. Randy Yates, the buyer's son-in-law, unfolded his lanky self from the driver's seat. Two men looking a whole lot like bookends crawled from the back doors, come to look over Raines's investment. It figured a man who'd spend that sort of money on a ranch wouldn't set foot there hisself.

Mark peered over his coffee cup and hollered them up to the house. "Have some coffee and we'll saddle up and you can take a look at the place." As if they hadn't already seen it. No one bought a pig in a poke if they had any sense.

"You surely have a pickup or vehicle. I don't ride in anything that needs a saddle." Yates shook out the wrinkles in his pants.

Jones looked like he'd been goosed but held back a laugh. He'd once referred to the buyer, Raines, as a six-foot-two prick. The only other man he'd ever listed in that special class was a movie director who made him drive a herd of ranch cattle down the same valley twenty times.

Mark eyed the sharp-creased britches and white shirts the three wore and wished like hell he could seat them on the backs of his horses, but maybe he ought not to do that. "We can take the Jimmy, but the seat won't hold us all so them fellas can ride in the bed."

In the end, they rode out in the Caddy, Yates cringing aloud every time it bottomed out on the ranch roads. He acted much like a kid checking out his latest new toy. Surely, he was older than he acted.

Under the circumstances, Mark figured he could forego calling Raines any sort of names. A few hours later, the Caddy, now covered in a thick layer of dust, departed. Mark and Jones waved goodbye from the yard. Both dissolved into near hysterical laughter, pounded each other on the back and went inside to pour up two glasses of lemonade. The generator meant drinks were cold and these were a welcome reprieve.

———

DIRTY SHIRT JONES'S NAME WAS soon on the deed to the farm down in Lehi.

Since he didn't drink, the best way he could take his mind off leaving the ranch and his memories of the early days him and Alma and Jones spent developing the land was to get hisself busy on the new ranch down in Paradise Valley. He was setting a crew to fencing the place and installing a cattle guard. Before they sold the big ranch, he made Sam cut him out the best dozer of the two. For three hundred dollars, he had it hauled down to the valley for his use. Sam paid the bill and Mark promised to run it for him if he ever needed the use of one. Mark kept three horses he considered his own. They and some of Jones's mounts went to the Lehi farm until fencing and water drilling were completed.

Yates told them he knew enough about the deal to run the ranch Raines had bought. He never offered to keep the three cowboys Mark had employed up there, so Mark found them jobs with another rancher who knew what good workers they'd been. Rosita moved to her daughter's house in Buckeye and he paid her wages until he got a trailer set up for her. He'd bunk at the new place till he decided on building a house there, but he would bring in some trailers for the movie folks should that deal come about. To his mind, he'd settled all the loose ends of his old life and was ready to start a new one. The hardest thing to put behind him were memories of Alma, but he kept trying hard.

Jones came up to see how he was getting along and caught up with Mark supervising the delivery of the house trailer.

Scratching his head, Jones eyed the goings-on. "No telling what you'll be up to next. Reckon you got something up your sleeve for that." He gestured at the men leveling one of the trailers.

"Making plans for some movie companies. Going to shoot movies out here and those people need a place to be between takes."

"Last I heard, you'd gone off to the rodeo. Nothing like staying busy. You make me look like a snake on a cold day, just barely wiggling along."

Before Mark could reply, a drilling rig rolled noisily up the road, parked a few yards away, and the driver hopped out.

"Mister Shaw?"

"That's me. Let me show you where to start." He turned to Jones who tagged along behind, boots kicking up dust and mumbling about Mark's goings-on. "Had that old man from down south of Tempe to witch for water." He stopped at a stick with a flag tied on it. "Right here. He claims there's water."

The driller nodded and without a word hiked to his rig. A helper jumped down and directed the driver to back up to the spot.

"I don't reckon you have anything much to do, so maybe you'd like to come down to my place and help me with that horse we broke to ride. He just plain won't pull a plow." Jones slapped his thigh and he-hawed.

"Naw, I thought in my spare time I'd get involved in rodeoing again. I've bought shares in a company."

Jones stopped and stared goggle-eyed at him. "I swear if you don't beat all."

"Gotta stay busy. Life don't wait around for a fellow to catch up. First thing you know, it'll have come and gone. Let's go on up to the bunk house and get a drink of something cold."

Seated in the shade of a stand of junipers, he poured from a thermos and the two visited to the accompanying roar and thud of the drilling rig and the shouts of the men placing the trailers.

"I'm seriously thinking of getting back into rodeoing."

"Well, yeah, you said."

Mark stared out across the valley. No matter how far he looked, that was his land. It was a pleasant thought. But still not enough. Not the movie making or the ranching or the rodeoing could fill the hole in his life. A pretty woman rode out there in the heat waves rising from the pastures. A woman he couldn't lay hold of, no matter how hard he tried. Damn, would he ever get over Alma? He shook himself back into the present.

"No, I mean bronc riding, bulldogging, and the like."

Jones sucked at his teeth. "I should not say this, but aren't you too old to go doing that sort of stuff? Hell, man, you could break a leg."

"I could break a leg riding out across the ranch, but that don't mean I'm not going to do it."

Work on the well proceeded pretty dang good till the driver of the drilling rig chased him down when he was in the corral wiping down the sorrel he'd had out most of the day checking the progress of the fencing.

Charlie, who was in charge of the well drilling, frowned and gazed down at his dusty work boots. "You remember our first hole come up dry?"

Mark nodded, hooked his thumbs in the loops of his waist band. "Yep. What's wrong?"

"Sorry boss, but we've gone deep enough we ought to've hit if it's there. 'Fraid your witcher may not be too good."

Mark raised his brows and stared past Charlie. "Let's give it one more try, then maybe we'll have to find us a better witcher. Heard this 'ole boy was tops."

Charlie spit between his boots. "There's a good growth of grass a ways lower than this last one. Still might have set the witcher's stick to jumping. Something's setting it off."

"Okay. It's getting late. Call it a day and come back in the morning. We have to get good water out here."

Charlie nodded. "See you then."

The next day, Mark was riding back in for supper when he heard a whoop and holler from down at the ranch.

Kicking the sorrel into a gallop, he arrived in time to see water spreading over the ground. Boots caked in mud, Charlie gave him a big grin. "Appears just in the edge. I'll put down one more drilling yonder if you want. It'll plumb blow I'd bet." He pointed below where he stood.

Mark watched the steady stream from the pipe sticking up out of the ground and nodded in agreement. The next day, they hit a gusher of an artesian, sending water twenty feet or more into the air. Whooping and hollering brought all the hands already quitting for the day racing out to stand under the spray till their clothes were dripping. Laughing, Mark tossed his sweat-soaked hat into the air and joined them. Before full dark, Charlie and his men had a plug installed and the flow shut down. He handed Mark the wrench.

He stood there holding it while the drilling rig turned around and drove off, taillights disappearing into the night. One less thing to stew about.

The following Saturday, Sam drove out to see his progress and beat his leg with his hat when Mark wrenched opened the fireplug on the real good well. Water flew out twenty feet and he looked shocked.

"You are the luckiest guy I know, Mark Shaw."

Mark eyed the water for a minute. "Sam, sell me the forty north of here. It's downhill from here. I could sure use the water coming out of that underground aquifer. Gotta be a lake down there."

"All right. Come by and I'll go you one better and sell you that eighty. You know I paid two dollars an acre for this damn land in a tax auction in 1942."

"Aw, Sam—" He put his hand on the man's shoulder and headed him for the palm-covered squaw shade where Rosita stood in her white apron ready to serve them sun tea. "—we ain't seen anything in this country yet."

"You know Mark, you're right."

"I'm building a movie set. Folk are saying TV is going to be the place to be."

The tea was cold, thanks to the generator making ice in the fridge. Comfortable in the shade, a gentle summer breeze fanned their hair.

Sam lowered his bare head and shook it. "No, son. TV is black and white. They can't make it like Technicolor. TV don't stand a chance. Any actor gets on it they won't let him be in another movie again. It won't be more than radio with pictures."

"It damn sure ain't hurting Hopalong Cassidy. He's a bigger star now than when he made those movies he happened to own."

"Boyd was broke when they found him and his library of films. Nice story. But I think that was like the ranch you found for us. What works once stops working soon as everything is bought up. We could'a had others, but when folks heard what we did they went and bought every last one, because they knew about them and we didn't move fast enough."

"That proves you're wrong about TV. Works once, it'll work again. I'm watching one right now. Some guy who used to be in Hoppie's movies. He's shooting those serials at Cudiah Studios in Scottsdale. *26 Men.* It's about the Arizona Rangers."

Sam couldn't be convinced. "He's kidding himself. He can't hope to compete with Hollywood."

"Sam, I'd bet you that he makes it."

"Fine, you pay me forty bucks an acre for that land. He makes it big, I'll give you your money back."

"That's a deal." Mark stuck out his hand and they shook on it.

Sam looked around for a TV antenna. "Them bed springs on that windmill get you TV out here?"

"That and the surplus generator I bought down at the Air Force base."

"You are a dandy, Mark Shaw. We need to be in more deals together."

"Don't you have land out by Superstition Mountain?"

Sam looked out across the valley. "Sure. What do you need that for?"

"To rent it to a movie company. Glen Ford is going to make a movie about the Lost Dutchman mine."

Sam laughed. "You got a deal. I want halvers."

"Better than forty percent. All right, it's a deal. We'll make fifteen thousand and they'll leave the set they build on it."

Sam dropped his chin. "Man, are you on the ball. How did you get that?

"You remember Linda?"

"Oh, hell yes."

"She sent me the whole deal and told me who to contact."

Sam smiled. "You still got that picture I had framed from *Life* of you and her?"

"Damn right. I wouldn't trade it for anything."

"I never could believe you didn't steal her."

Mark shook the notion away. "I always appreciated how you set me up with her. But she lives in a different world than I do."

"I was jealous as hell of you. I knew you hadn't simply let her slip through your hands."

Mark smiled. "You were lucky you didn't score with her, pardner. Bet she'd have killed you."

They both laughed. In the end, Sam had to repay him the money for the eighty acres. *26 Men* made the producer a fortune in one year. Mark leveled the eighty acres and planted alfalfa, making a sixty-forty split with a farmer from near Tempe to irrigate and bale it on the shares. By the time he was involved in the rodeo, he had stacks of hay that Rosita sold for him by the bale or ton.

———

THAT NEXT YEAR, LONNIE GRAIG asked him to help supply stock for the big Phoenix Rodeo when he dropped by one of Mark's shows. Lonnie wanted to rent his roping steers and a set of calves, plus have him to supply hay for all the stock at Phoenix.

"We can do that." He went on down to the chute to put the bareback rigging on his horse.

Amazed, Lonnie watched him. "Damn, I heard you still rode at some of these shows. Didn't believe it, but you really do. I want to watch. I loved that picture of you and that movie star hugging before the chutes in *Life*."

"That was kinda pulled over on me." He laughed, recalling it. "As long as getting on a horse is still fun, I'll do it. Even without a pretty woman to hug."

"Let me help you pull that riggin'."

"Sure, but you ain't half as good looking as she was."

Lonnie smiled. "You ever see her again?"

"Yeah, we keep in touch."

"I'll be damned. You've had quite a life for starting out as a sharecropper's son."

"That got me ready for life." He was set and nodded. The gate swung back hard. Snowball saw his break and went out flying. The big white gelding really gave him a ride, and after the pickup man let him down, he threw his hat across the arena and the crowd roared.

"Eighty-one," Carl Franks announced.

He came back over the chutes and Lonnie shook his head.

"You may not be Jim Shoulders or Jack Bushbom, but they better be glad that you aren't pulling the circuit."

Mark dismissed it and they went to watch the show for a while before the dogging event. He missed the steer when he shied and ate some dirt but was no worse off. At the same rodeo, some tall girl from Sonata was all he heard about—a barrel racer, on a stout bay horse he liked, who came in third. That was all he knew about her.

It had been a dozen years since his discharge when he helped his buddies put on the Phoenix Grand Championship Rodeo. A girl he thought must be a teenager, who stood damn near six feet tall, was entered in the queen contest. A powerful horsewoman, she kept crossing his path all week long behind the scenes until he decided this business was not accidental.

It was midafternoon before the third performance and she'd already driven the bulldogging steers up the alleyway from the back pens before he had a chance to even saddle his horse.

"This what you were going after?" she asked him, reining her great horse back and forth to keep the Mexican cattle bunched at the gate to go on to where they'd be penned for the night's event.

"That's fine. But sister, I've been stumbling over you all week. Tell me why I'm the one you're herding."

With a big open grin, she rested her hands and reins on the saddle horn, "You really want to know?"

"Yeah, I'm a big boy. Tell me."

"I think you're an exciting guy. Not many guys your age ride broncs, and still bulldog. I love rodeoing. I like to be around rodeo and their people, but I'm not going to sleep in an old car's backseat and eat baloney sandwiches with these younger guys to get to enjoy my favorite sport. I found out you don't have a woman. Besides, you're tall enough I won't have to bend over to dance with you."

He blinked in disbelief. "Wait—Old. *Me?* I'm just getting started." But she was right. She might be twenty-one, and would soon tire of him. But by dang, she was a good-looking woman and he was about set on looking around.

She blushed some under her suntan, briefly looked away, then came back with her words for him. "I wouldn't mind much. They tell me I look a lot younger than I am. What do you say?"

"Good God, sister, you don't even know me. But maybe we could go dancing after the last show? I promise I'm not dangerous."

She grinned, and the horse danced under her. The material of the tailored silk shirt she wore clung to her body.

He wanted to find out more about her. She was, after all, in this business and dang good at it. It was more than time he looked around for a good woman or grow old and grizzly.

She grinned, and dimples danced on her cheeks. "I think you're just tall enough to suit me."

"Tall enough? You judge men by their height?"

"When they ask me to go dancing. No danger I'd be looking down at the top of your head."

"I'll be danged if you aren't something. I'd like a chance to prove that there's more to me than being tall."

"Guess we'd better pen these longhorns first." She indicated the bulldogging cattle before her and her horse.

"Yes, take them up there to the pen marked number five. You know I won't be able to get out of here until after the bull riding tonight. But we can talk then or go ahead and go dancing if you've made up your mind I'm safe." He still had his doubts. Was she simply putting him on?

"Oh, so I get an opening in your schedule." She rocked her head from side to side. "I accept."

"Do you drink?" he asked as she rode by him.

She twisted in the saddle. "I'm over twenty-one."

He really did not believe her about that, but it meant she could get in the

Paradise Ball Room. They always had lots of Bob Wills music in that place to dance to. He shook his head. Why did this rodeo queen want him? That baloney sandwich business in the backseat of an old car deal wasn't too far from the truth for cowboys starting out in rodeoing.

But if she really was serious, he'd have to make some changes. He'd been a bachelor way too long and had developed a few bad habits, living-wise. *Was* she serious? She'd be a great threat to his own sanity. He realized he didn't even know her name.

She came back short-loping her great horse though the arena. He held the gate open for her. No way this deal between them would ever come off. She was too good looking to come around wanting him. Conscious of his own appearance, he shoved his shirttail in behind his back.

"What'd you like to be called the best?" Only way to find out her name without outright asking.

"Julie."

"Julie... That's what I'll call you. We've got to cut those roping calves out next. I've got the list of the ones we need for tonight." He tracked down the wide alleyway after her. They used the wide lane to feed the stock hay off his truck bed.

Ahead of him, she was dismounted at the right pen, pulling down her tight pants that must have rode up on her.

"Where did you get that good steeldust horse?" He admired the fine animal.

"How do you know he's a steeldust?" Her clear blue eyes looked hard at him for an answer.

"Maybe just a guess." He winked. Weren't many of them left and he knew one from across the lot.

She broke up laughing. "They told me that you were tough, gruff, and honest, but I like the funny part the best."

He settled tight in the saddle and studied her seriously. Maybe, just maybe. Only time and lots of consideration would tell. He wasn't about to tie up with someone who might break his heart. He'd already had that once.

10

THE FIRST TIME HE TOOK her in his arms on the dance floor that night, he had this sense of them belonging together, though he hoped he wasn't getting too far ahead of himself. Looking down into her closed eyes, he missed a step but just managed to avoid tromping on her toes.

Take it easy buddy. He had to make sure this is what he wanted. More importantly—what *she* wanted, too. Go slow.

"You sure look pretty with all the horsehair and dust cleaned off."

She snuggled a bit closer. "Thank you. You don't clean up so bad yourself."

With that out of the way, where did he go from here? It'd been a long time since he'd courted a woman and that one hadn't worked out so well. He wondered where Sheila was and what she was doing. He didn't really care, but it was a passing thought to take his mind off Julie's body, so close to his. With Alma, they had just fallen in together. No need for all the proper stuff.

"If you'd like, we could go out to Bloody Basin Sunday. It's not too far by car and the road is passable. I don't own it anymore, but we could pay Yates a visit. I'm sure he wouldn't mind showing off his toy."

"Sounds great, but I'd rather ride out. And what's this about his toy? Something special or is it a joke?"

"He's the son-in-law that was given the ranch to keep him occupied, so he treats it like his favorite toy, instead of a serious enterprise. If Raines doesn't keep an eye on him, he's liable to run it down. As to riding out, it's a hard three days on horseback."

She grinned up at him. "Too hard for an old man, or can't your ranch do without you that long?"

"Maybe a little of both? No, really. It's not something I have time to do till we get the alfalfa crop in and baled, then see the fields turned up, then there's fall branding of calves and—"

She held up a hand to stop him. "So, it's going to be that way. Work comes first, fun comes second... or is it last?"

The music ended, and he took her back to their table, one arm around her waist. The muscles beneath his touch were strong. He pulled back her chair, then slid into his own, unable to take his eyes off her. No good for her to think he'd let work come before her, but it had always been the only thing—till now.

She did look pretty, her long mahogany hair tied up in a twist, allowing a few curls to hang around her face. The sparkles on her eyelids glittered under the rotating lights—and oh, those azure blue eyes. With the sweaty longneck in her hand and his icy Coke glass before him, he gazed in wonderment like some lovestruck kid.

He searched for something to talk about to keep from drooling. Finally, he came up with something. "I saw you in Casa Grande on that great steeldust horse."

"My parents have a ranch at Sonata. I still live there."

"They know you're here with me?"

She blushed. "I'm not ashamed to be here with you."

"I didn't intend to make you blush about it. I'm Mark Nobody. Why does a good looking, sober young woman come around and want me?"

"Haven't made up my mind yet. I mean about wanting you." She raised the bottle and took a sip, watching him around the glass.

"Maybe you ought to make up your mind, then."

"Give me time. Meanwhile, let's spend some time together. You might be an old grouch."

"Hell, you might snore." The minute he said it, he wanted to take it back. Stupid to assume such a thing so soon.

She got the giggles and almost choked on the beer. When she could speak, she did. "Don't count on finding that out anytime soon."

The following Friday, he drove down to Sonata to see her and meet her folks. That didn't go as good as he had hoped.

Her dad met him on the front verandah. The house was a large, two-story structure surrounded by shrubs covered in blooms. He didn't know what they were, but he wanted some out at the ranch. They had plenty of water with the artesian well. It'd be something to talk about. Women liked discussing flowers.

He introduced himself, which is how he finally learned Julie's last name.

"Bryce Conroy," her father announced.

"Julie will be right out, but I wanted us to get acquainted first. We could sit." He indicated chairs beneath a fall of purple blooms overhead. "You own a ranch up in Paradise Valley, I understand. You been in ranching long?"

"Well, I began working on it soon as I got out of the army when the war ended, so you could say so. Sold the first one after developing it and selling off most of the wild herds running up there at Bloody Basin."

"Seems like I've heard of that one. That Raines guy bought it a year or so ago."

Mark nodded. "That's when I sold out and came down to the valley to the land I'd bought before I went in the service."

"Mark Shaw." Conroy snapped his fingers. "You're the man who's getting in with the movie people to film on your place. How's that going for you?"

"I'm just getting started but I think it'll pan out for me."

He shook his head. "Running with that movie bunch has to be—uh, well, a bit dangerous."

"Dangerous? I don't get it."

"Drinking, carousing. Well, you surely understand what I'm getting at."

So that was it. The man was trying to figure if Mark was good enough for his daughter. Was he going to take her to dangerous places? He wasn't surprised. He'd expected it. He tamped down his temper. "Your daughter is safe with me, Mr. Conroy. I don't drink, and I don't carouse, whatever that's intended to mean."

The older man's eyes grew hard as flint. "Julie is quite a bit younger than you, it would appear, and you've been around, being in the army and all. I just don't want her hurt in any way."

The screen door popped open and a fiery-eyed Julie stepped out on the porch. "Are you ready to go, Mark?"

She never even looked at her father.

He wasn't sure whether to say yes or no. He had a reply for the man and hated to leave without giving it. After all, he wasn't a young wet-behind-the-ears suitor. But that was Conroy's main objection to him—what he wasn't. Perhaps it was better if his reply went unsaid. For now, anyway.

In the robin's egg blue Chevy he'd bought new a few months earlier, he settled a mad-as-a-wet-hen Julie in the passenger side and went around to climb in, remaining silent till then.

"Okay. First thing I need to know is, just how old are you, anyway?"

"Old enough to make my own decisions and choose my own man."

"That won't do. I need to know for sure before this goes any farther. Does your dad have any say in what you do? I can't be dating some underage gal. It just won't do."

"Well, I can tell you I'm not underage, whatever you consider that to be."

"It isn't what I consider, damn it. It's what it is." He slammed on the brakes and pulled off the road. "Tell me now, or I'm taking you home. I'm serious about us, Julie, and I want to keep seeing you. Now, just how do you feel? Be honest with me."

Instead of answering him, she scooted in the seat till her knee touched the gearshift, stretched up, and kissed him on the jaw. "There. That's how serious I am. And I'm twenty-five, that's how old I am, and my dad is an old grump. He'll come around. Any more questions?"

For a full minute he sat stock still, then he turned, took her shoulders in both hands and kissed her, well and good, right on the mouth. And she kissed him back, well and good.

———

DESPITE HER FATHER'S OBJECTIONS, JULIE went to the ranch at Bloody Basin with Mark the following weekend, where they stayed for more than a week. Dirty Shirt Jones looked out for the ranch in the valley while they were gone.

In that hard, desolate country up by Bloody Basin, he learned something about Julie that surprised him.

They were sitting around a campfire, bundled up close together since it was getting cold in high country. He asked her why she was so quick to start seeing him after they met.

Silent for a while, she played with a stick in the fire. "It was that picture in *Life* Magazine. You looked so carefree, so confident, with your arms around that pretty actress."

"Linda Acosta?"

"Yes, her."

"But why would that matter to you?"

"I was nineteen years old—a sophomore at U of A dreaming of rodeoing. I'd barrel-raced in the small rodeos since I was sixteen. Seeing you made me wild to be that girl in your arms, but I wanted to be a rodeo queen, not a movie star. I wanted you and me to perform in the Phoenix rodeo and had dreams about that happening. Then I saw you in person and there I was, a rodeo queen. It was just too perfect, too much of what I had dreamed. So, I decided to make my dream come true."

While she talked, he listened with amazement. "So, you set out to lasso me?"

She laid her head on his shoulder. "I hope you don't mind. I know the man is the one who should do the lassoing, but I couldn't help it. You were so cute in those boots and spurs, I couldn't resist. I was actually jealous."

He hugged her close, then wrestled her to her back on the ground. "Cute in my boots and spurs, huh?"

Her laughter echoed across the hills and somewhere, off in the distance, a coyote howled.

By the time they came back from Bloody Basin, Mark wanted to marry her. Conroy was furious and glared bullets at him when he brought her home. She told him not to mind her daddy, but he had no choice. He knew better than to push it till he could get on the good side of the man. Splitting a family was not a good idea and he wanted the marriage to work. It was the main reason he'd made up to his own dad and loved his step-brothers and sister even though it hurt when he had married again after his mom died. Family was too danged important to him to divide Julie's. He'd by damn get along with her old man or die trying.

He knew they had to talk about it, he just didn't look forward to it. He just couldn't come up with something, and fall was fast approaching. Not much changed in the valley, but the mountaintops showed early snowfalls. When the wind was right, there was a touch of winter in the air. Nights became cooler and a fire felt good. He'd built a bunkhouse first thing at the ranch, but there still wasn't a house. If he was to get serious about him and Julie, he needed to have a place for her to live. It would also show Bryce Conroy he was serious about his intentions.

When Dirty Shirt came to visit, Mark told him about his plans to build a house.

"Looks comfortable right here to me." Dirty Shirt peered around the bunkhouse. "Congratulations, though. I'm happy to hear you have finally found a woman to love."

He became the first to know about Mark's desire to marry Julie. It was just like Jones to have something to say about it. "Well, it seems like you better get busy then. Does she know about this?"

"Maybe. I've made it pretty plain."

"Takes more than plain with some women."

"Her old man detests me. I can't come between them. This is crazy. Since the war, everything I've tried has come about. Never have I failed. Not with the ranches or the rodeoing. We've got water where there was none. Hell, I'm almost rich."

Dirty Shirt chuckled. "One cannot be almost-rich. One is rich, or he is not."

"Well, I guess I'm not."

"It matters only who you ask. I think you are rich and many others do too. What is wrong with this man that he does not think so?" Upset, Jones rose and poked the fire so hard sparks went everywhere.

"Don't burn the place down with that poking. He is more than almost. He is way rich."

"You white people. Almost rich, way rich, just rich. It is crazy. Perhaps if you worked as hard with this problem as you do with others, you could bring about this marriage."

"I'm trying. Believe me. Funny you can give marrying advice when you still ain't come up with a woman for yourself."

"I ain't been trying that hard, my friend. It would appear you are not trying hard enough, either."

So, on his friend's opinion, Mark started trying harder.

He'd once heard that the best place to begin when trying to impress a future father-in-law is to give him a chance to mingle in your world, to meet some important people you knew. So Mark planned a barbecue for Labor Day weekend. He invited Raines and his family, Sam of course—'cause he was even richer than Conroy—and Dirty Shirt, because he was a friend and it was important to remember friends even when one was rich. He called Linda, asking her to come and bring some of the movie people she knew. He made sure Julie knew they should behave themselves and explained his reasoning behind saying so. This would show Conroy just how ordinary they were, despite their unearned reputations.

Of course, they were all rich. He invited people who had built their businesses because of his efforts, like Noah Gaines. He bought thick steaks, black caviar, and had fresh shrimp, crab, and lobster brought in. He also hired a chef and a couple of young boys in white shirts to serve food and drinks. Mark didn't drink anything but lemonade, tea, and Cokes, but he consulted Linda about supplying the best in malt liquor, bourbon, and vodka, as well as some other drinks he'd never heard of. He cautioned he not to invite anyone who was a drunkard, though.

Almost everyone in the county was invited. It turned out that Arizona senator, Coin Hayden, was a friend of Linda's and he sent an RSVP. It so happened he would be in the state during that time and he would be pleased to attend. If this did not impress Conroy and make him realize what a catch Mark was for his daughter, then nothing would.

A few days before the event, when preparations were in full swing, Mark went to Dirty Shirt with his concerns.

"What if no one comes? What if Conroy turns down my invitation? Maybe the shrimp will arrive spoiled. What if Julie changes her mind and doesn't want to marry me? After all, I haven't asked her yet."

Dirty Shirt sat and patiently listened to all of his friend's concerns, shaking his head in wonderment. "How can a man who has the golden touch be so worried about such a thing as a little cookout?"

"Golden touch? Little cookout?" Mark rose from his chair and paced round and round, practically banging into walls in the small bunkhouse. "Fifty people have accepted their invitations. I have spent nearly four thousand dollars on this little cookout. My touch better be golden, whatever that means."

Dirty Shirt's eyes bugged out and, for a moment, it looked to Mark like he had silenced the outspoken man. But he hadn't. His friend had an answer for everything. "Then perhaps you should act like it."

The final straw came three nights before the big blowout event, when he and Julie went to the movies in town. On the way home, he decided to take Dirty Shirt's advice and act like a rich man throwing a big party.

"Have you seen the list of people coming to my barbecue?"

"No, but I know they're from all over the county."

"Excellent."

"What are you doing, Mark?"

"What do you mean?"

"In all the months I've known you and we've dated, you've never acted snobbish. Now, all of a sudden you are doing everything you can to impress all these so-called important people. Why?"

He pulled over, afraid he'd wreck the truck if he let out the head of steam he'd built up over her question. "I'm doing it for you. For us. Don't you understand?"

"Hmm. I guess I don't. A big party is *not* what I wanted—especially when you're only inviting all these bigwigs and ignoring others. Like Rosita, and Charlie. All the others who have helped you along the way but aren't considered rich and famous."

He hammered at the steering wheel. Gawdamn if he'd ever figure out women. Couldn't she see what was going on? What he was trying to do? He'd tell her so if he wasn't so blamed frustrated. Infuriated. All those other words that meant failure to understand.

"Mark, please. Don't be angry with me. I think the party will be a lot of fun. I just question your reason for having it. You are trying to impress my father, and I get that. But you know what would really impress him?"

"No." He sputtered out the word. "Please tell me."

"Take me home. Come in and sit down with him and tell him that you love his daughter and would be pleased if he would get off his damn high horse and accept that fact."

"And have him knock my block off? No, sir."

"Not true. What he respects is men who stand up to trouble and never back down. You have let him bumfuzzle you."

Mark stared at her as if she had come from New York City. "Do you mean I've spent four thousand dollars for nothing?"

She turned to look at him, staring for close to a minute. Laughter built in her chest and rumbled out like a volcano erupting. "Leave it to you. I love you, Mark Shaw, but sometimes you do the dumbest things. I'm not some buckle bunny after the richest or most famous cowboy on the circuit. You can't impress me, and neither can you impress my father with money. He was a miner as a young man and he got what he has the same way you did. With grit and determination and a will to never give up. He likes people who are like that. So, show him that side of you."

A knot swelled in his throat.

God, he was an idiot.

"Don't look so stricken. I think this barbecue is a fabulous idea. Why not tell my father tonight that you intend to announce our engagement there and you hope he will still attend? And be firm. That is—if you still want to marry me."

"I've wanted to marry you since I first saw you. It's just been the only thing I've run up against that I couldn't manage to get. I'll gladly try it your way if you'll promise me you won't break my heart."

"I'll gladly promise that. I'll be by your side till we're old and gray."

He took her in his arms and kissed her face all over till she giggled with delight. Then he took her home to face her father down.

Lights burned in the downstairs rooms when Mark pulled up and cut the ignition. He couldn't just let her out. He had to go inside and get this settled. She opened her own door, stepped out, and slammed it. He cringed. If her father was asleep, that surely had awakened him. The way the windows glowed, the entire family was up. He had no idea how her mother felt about him. He'd never met the woman. For some reason, Bryce had seen to that.

Julie curled an arm through his when he started toward the front door. "I'm right here with you. You're not doing this alone."

He gripped her hand against his body. "You sure about this? Absolutely sure?"

"Couldn't be more so. I love you."

The words went straight through to his heart, making it beat like a drum.

"I love you, too, but that wasn't what I meant. Are you sure this is the way to handle your father? I don't want to lose you."

"Whatever comes of this, you are not going to lose me. I promise. I always get what I want, same as you do. That should guarantee our success."

She led him up the steps and opened the door, pulling him inside behind her. "Come on. Don't back down now. I can't believe a man who's accomplished all you have can be so nervous about such a thing."

But he was. He hadn't been so nervous since the day he stepped off the ship to face the enemy. Bryce might as well be holding a gun to his head.

"Julie?" Her dad's voice rumbled out into the foyer. "Send that young man in here and go upstairs to bed."

She frowned, then smiled at him. "I'll go in with you if you'd like. I won't abandon you to him."

He patted her hand. "No, you go on up. It's best if you don't have to hear this."

She kissed his cheek and at the same time Bryce roared. "Mr. Shaw, *now* if you please."

"Where is he?" He whispered, so Bryce wouldn't hear.

With one hand on his back, she guided him toward an open door a few steps down the long hallway. "Good luck. We'll elope if necessary."

Oh, God. What was he going to do?

Well, she was behind him, whatever he did, so he took a deep breath and stepped through the doorway, shaking in his boots. How could a grown man feel so much like a complete fool?

Well, he did.

"Mr. Conroy? I'm here."

"I see that. I trust you and my daughter had a good time tonight."

"Yes sir, we did. I'm here to ask you—no, I'm here to *tell* you that I intend to marry your daughter, whether you like it or not." There, he had it out and it didn't look like the man was going to shoot him.

"Is that so? And where will you live? In that sorry bunkhouse on your ranch?"

"No, sir. I'm building us a house there. It's already in the works."

"And all this so soon. You don't even know each other that well, though I suppose you may have gotten better acquainted spending a week together. My daughter is a good girl. I won't have her reputation sullied by you or any other man."

"I would not dream of hurting her. She loves me and I love her. I want your blessing so we can announce our engagement at the barbecue Saturday. But we will get married, whether you like it or not. I want our families to remain friendly, but I want Julie more."

Conroy leaned back in his leather recliner, pinning Mark with a hard stare. "Is that so? Well, I don't like it one bit, but I can see you're set on this. I don't suppose I can stop you. She's as hard-headed as you. You and her can do what you please at that damned barbecue, but my wife and I will be out of town that weekend. I will not be there to see such nonsense. Now, if you don't mind, I've had my say and it appears you've had yours. Close the door on your way out."

Furious, Mark stomped out and slammed the front door as hard as he could. The old fool hadn't uttered his daughter's name one time during the entire conversation.

11

THAT DAMN FOOLISH OLD MAN. How could he be willing to lose her to get his own way?

Mark stopped in Lehi to call Julie, but the phone just kept ringing. Conroy probably didn't let her have one in her room, even though she was a grown woman. He finally hung up and drove on out to the ranch, tires spitting gravel and dirt. There was no way around that stubborn old man, and Mark could not give up Julie. First thing the next morning, he went to Phoenix to pick out her rings. Maybe he should've taken her, but he'd rather surprise her. Besides, there was still no answer down in Sonata. No matter what, he would have them before the barbecue. The engagement ring came in a set and the jeweler promised he would size them if they didn't fit, so he bought both. She would marry him despite her father. Hadn't she said so?

Still, Saturday morning came, and no one answered the phone. Mark slammed down the receiver. He had to get himself one of those so he didn't have to come to Lehi to make a call. Time to get back to the ranch to help Rosita herd those boys into shape, and make sure all the orders for food had arrived and were on ice. She'd be there. He had to believe that. He had chairs to get set up. He'd hired a crew, but someone had to keep order just the same.

One thing he couldn't bear was disorder. Everything in its place and finished on time. No sense in it being any other way.

By noon, cars and trucks were coming in a long line. Two of the crew made sure they were parked in an orderly fashion. His eyes continued to sweep over the arrivals, searching for Julie.

Dirty Shirt Jones brought along a couple of his cowboys to help with the heavy work. In the midst of the hubbub, Jones showed up out of nowhere to stand beside Mark.

He touched his elbow. "You look overwrought. Something wrong?"

"I'm worried about Julie. She should be here." In his mind was that day he'd waited for Alma and all he got was someone riding up to tell him she was dead. The vision wouldn't stop replaying itself. "What if something happened to her?"

Jones looked worried. "I could run down to Lehi, give her a call."

Mark shook his head. "I came up from there an hour ago. No one answers. I get a feeling her dad took her away somewhere. I've got everything I ever set out to get. Suppose I'm going to have to pay for that by losing her? First Alma, now Julie. I can't lose her, Jones. I just can't."

"She will come. I will just bet she is on her way right now. That is why she does not answer on the telephone."

A long black limousine emerged from the line of cars amidst a noisy welcome. Senator Hayden had arrived and, just behind him, two more impressive cars parked and unloaded Linda and the other movie people. Their arrival caused laughter and shouts and greetings from those who were already milling about, visiting and clamoring to be noticed by everyone who was important.

About then, Mark began to wish he'd never planned this gathering. What good would it do now anyway? He couldn't announce his and Julie's engagement. How could he enjoy anything without her here?

Someone grabbed his arm and he turned. Linda stood there, her beauty outshining all the others now lining up to fill their plates and find a place to sit. Delicious smells filled the air. Roasting meats, vegetables of every variety, baking bread, all being served from the portable grills brought in and set up last night.

She threw her arms around Mark and planted a kiss on his cheek. "Well, this is quite something you're throwing here. It's good to see you. You look fit." She pounded him on the arm.

He hugged her, hanging on too long and feeling sorry for himself. He managed a mumbled greeting, telling her how pretty she was.

"I hear great news is afoot. Where is the lucky lady?"

All he wanted to do was run away. When Senator Hayden finally stole Linda for a publicity shot, he escaped to the outer corral and stood there, leaning on the fence and staring out across the pasture. Off in the distance, almost too far to make out their markings, a herd of wild horses grazed as if nothing was going on. He fetched a pair of binoculars from the tack shed and swung them around to study the mustangs. Next week, maybe he and Dirty Shirt would go out and track them, bring back a few new additions to train for their remuda. It would take his mind off what he couldn't have.

He was about to turn the glasses to study late arrivals at the party when a long-legged yellow mare walked into sight, mane waving in the wind. It was like a shot in a movie, like she had posed and said, "Here I am. Come and get me."

Lord, she was beautiful.

He drew in a deep breath, then nearly gasped aloud when, at her side, appeared a blue roan colt, prancing on its toes. A desperate need suddenly welled up within Mark. A need for the beautiful mare and her colt.

Somehow, they were a sign that everything would be okay.

A foolish thing to believe, he knew, but he couldn't help it. He just knew he would have his Julie, just like he would have that blue roan colt. Both were meant for him. All he had to do was go after them like he had everything else he wanted.

Behind him, someone shouted with laughter. The mare's head came up and she spooked, took off at a run, the colt right behind her. My God, the beauty of the two of them running to catch up with the rest of the herd. It was about time for them to skedaddle, and so they did. Mark watched them gallop out of sight through the glasses.

Just as he went to take them back to the tack shed, someone touched his elbow.

Even before he turned around, he said her name. *Julie.* She smelled like fresh flowers and new cut leather. She wore jeans tucked into blue cowboy boots and a red and gold shirt with pearl buttons. No fancy dress and diamond necklace. Her long hair hung free past her shoulders, lifted by the wind to play around her lovely face. It was just her, Julie—the woman he needed above all else. Everything he'd ever wanted paled with the thought of having her. He let go of the glasses and they swung around his neck when he grabbed her, lifting her off her feet. Round and round he twirled her, laughing, kissing, nuzzling her throat, and kissing some more.

She kept saying his name and *I'm sorry,* over and over, but he flat out wasn't listening to much of anything but her name repeating in his head and in his heart.

Together, they leaned against the top rail, fingers entwined, talking one over the other. All he got out of it was the family had received a message that Conroy's mother was ill, and they had to go. She was okay now, this grandmother who almost messed up her granddaughter's life.

"Daddy says if I absolutely have to get engaged to that big dumb cowboy, then he won't try to stop it."

That, he heard loud and clear. It brought about another round of swinging, nuzzling, kissing and joy—pure joy.

Another voice cut into the melee. "Mark. Mark Shaw, you better introduce us. Is this the lucky lady?"

He sobered enough to study the pretty woman. Keeping Julie's hand, he introduced the two. "Julie Conroy, this is Linda Acosta."

The two sort of froze, their gazes taking a long toll of each other.

Linda broke the silence. "So, this is the mystery woman."

Julie appeared stunned for a moment, then she smiled real big. "And this is the lady from the magazine cover."

Linda took Julie's hand. "You better treat this big 'ol boy right. He's a keeper."

"Oh, you can bet your bottom dollar I will."

The two of them stood there, grinning silly-like at each other for a solid minute before they began to chatter like old friends.

Mark finally broke it up. "You know, I'm starving, and everything smells great. How about we fill our plates and sit somewhere so we can visit?"

By the time they settled at a table, others around them were joining the group, joking and telling stories.

It was finally time for Mark to make his big announcement. He stood, took Julie's hand, and rang a cowbell Dirty Shirt handed him with a sly grin. Everyone quieted and turned to see what was up. He stepped onto a table and took her hand to help her up there, too.

"Attention friends. I want to thank you all for coming out here for this real special event." He chuckled. "Oh, yeah, I know the food is good and all, but the real reason for this here gathering is to announce my engagement to this lovely lady, Julie Conroy. Can you believe she's actually promised to marry this old cowboy? I couldn't be happier."

He slipped the glittering diamond engagement ring onto her finger. It fit perfectly. Of course, what could Mark Shaw ever do wrong? He couldn't think of anything, now that he had the woman of his dreams.

Dirty Shirt whistled, and everyone cheered. Soon, people were milling about, congratulating him and shaking Julie's hands till they were numb.

Later, a band tuned up and played some good dance music. When it grew dark, dozens of lanterns were hung on cords, though a bright harvest moon shone on the festivities and couples danced into the night.

It must've been three a.m. before everyone drifted away toward home. Mark laughed so hard he couldn't breathe when Rosita came out, gave him a stern look, fetched Julie and took her to her trailer to sleep. He was still shaking his head in wonderment when he retired to the bunk house for the night.

That night, he dreamed of Julie astride a blue roan, the most beautiful pair he'd ever laid eyes on. When he awoke, he vowed to capture the second-best thing he'd ever wanted—that yellow mare and her blue roan colt.

———

WITH THE WEDDING SET FOR around the holidays, Mark got serious about getting the house built. He'd made an uneasy peace with Bryce Conroy, as he was acquainted with a contractor who could take care of whatever Julie and Mark wanted. The architect, John Deavers, had an office in Scottsdale where they toured some of his spaciously designed homes. They wanted a rambling Spanish *hacienda* with air conditioning, not swamp coolers. So, he'd been working on plans which included fireplaces and a swimming pool with a large area to entertain.

Julie gave him a wry smile. "Think they'll run a phone line out there?"

He nodded. "Sam can get one-hundred-ten volts out there. He can get the telephone company, too."

"So we can have electricity now, as well?"

"Of course. I went with propane heating. It's so cheap these days, you can't beat it unless you have natural gas." Mark shook his head. "I am not going for a pipeline out there."

The hands all departed for their homes to spend the holidays. Julie, Rosita, and Mark handled feeding the cattle and horses every day, breaking bales open from the back of his pickup and tossing the hay out of the pickup bed to the trailing animals. Rosita continued to guard Julie's virginity and the couple were forced to grab secret moments together as if they were teenagers. With fences in good shape, a constant supply of water, and the final alfalfa crop of the year cut and baled, there wasn't much more to do till cows and mares began to drop calves and foals in the spring. What there was, Julie and Mark could easily handle. She was every bit as tough and resilient as any man he'd ever known. And she loved the work. They were a perfect fit.

One night in the barn, hanging bridles in the tack room after a ride around the north pasture to assure the fences were all up, he turned to bump into her. The notion hit him that this was the woman who would soon be his wife. Their gazes locked, and he took her in his arms. She felt warm from the day's work, her hair tickling his cheek.

"You know how much I love you?" He kissed the nape of her neck. Lord she smelled good, work's sweat and all. "Where is our chaperone?"

"I think she's busy in the kitchen fixing supper."

"So, we have maybe five minutes before she rings that supper bell."

Julie tickled him. "I can hardly wait till we're in our own home."

"Yeah, me, too. She'll probably run over every night to keep an eye on what we're doing."

The bell clanged loud enough for folks on the adjoining ranch five miles away to hear.

He kissed her good and proper, ran fingers through her hair, and held her so close he could feel her heart beat. His breath quickened, as did hers, fanning hot against his neck.

The bell rang a second time.

"Time to get in there before she sends Jones out to find us." Reluctantly, Mark released her.

Hand in hand, they ran to the house where Rosita stood in the doorway, arms crossed over her ample bosom.

After supper, they retired to the living room where a fire burned in the fireplace. Jones had eaten in the bunkhouse with the hands and Rosita rattled around in the kitchen cleaning up.

Julie picked up a *Good Housekeeping* magazine from the table and relaxed beside Mark. He stretched out with his head in her lap. Rosita would finish up and wait to walk with Julie back to her trailer.

"I always wanted a plantation type house." Julie leafed through a magazine that showed floor plans and photos of finished homes. She'd took to staying with Rosita most every day. Between sharing the ranch work, planning their wedding, and picking a house plan, it made sense for her to be there rather than down in Sonata.

Mark hesitated on a page showing a low-constructed log home, sprawled all on one floor. She put a finger on the page. "I like this. It's so you and me. It looks like it belongs here on this ranch, where everything fits the lay of the land. It doesn't interrupt the exquisite beauty of Paradise Valley. What do you think?"

He was often caught up by her words and the way she pronounced some of them, soft and clinging. He was learning to think much like she did in certain ways and it made him feel more settled. Happier.

"I do like it a lot. We could be comfortable there, I think."

She dog eared the page and closed the magazine.

Rosita appeared, and Julie kissed him properly as far as their keeper was concerned and the two women left. He remained on the rug, staring into the fire, content with his life, filled now with only good memories. He'd finally put to rest the bad ones.

The next day, they finished all the regular chores by lunchtime.

"Rosita, why don't you take the rest of the day off? You spend all your time taking care of us and have none for yourself. We can handle things from here. We can even round up supper. You can come back tomorrow."

Rosita eyed him like a snake on a bird. "Will you promise me no funny stuff?"

Mark tossed a quick glance toward Julie and crossed his heart. "I promise."

Julie made the same promise.

"Well, okay then. But remember, God is watching you."

It was all Mark could do to keep from snorting with laughter. He nodded. "Yes, I know."

Arm in arm, they watched the plump woman hustle back to her trailer.

"She's such a dear woman."

Julie looked up at him. "Indeed, she is."

"You're beautiful." Mark kissed her on the nose.

She shook her finger sat him. "Remember what we promised. It's so pretty outside today. Everything is golden and silent, like it's pausing before anything happens. Let's go for a ride."

"That's a good idea." They put on sweaters, went to the barn for saddles and bridles, and walked out into the pasture with them. As if called, two of the geldings whinnied and raised their noses into the air as if testing their odor, then trotted to them. For some horses, a ride was as enjoyable as it was for those who rode them.

Once saddled and mounted, the animals burst into a gallop at the touch of heels against their flanks.

He hadn't seen the mare and her colt since the day of the barbecue, though each time he rode out for work, he looked for them. Today was no different. Once the horses had their joyful run, they slowed them to a walk.

"I hope we can spot the blue roan colt. I want you to see him and his mother. They are so beautiful. Maybe if we're quiet, we can sneak up on the pair and their band."

"When did you first see him?"

"A few weeks ago, just a glimpse and they were gone. I want that colt."

"The mare, too, I hope. They shouldn't be separated."

"Of course."

"It's amazing how the roans come about, isn't it?"

He glanced at her in surprise. "Not a lot of people know about them. It's a genetic anomaly."

"Well listen to you. Sounding like a scientist."

"Naw, just in awe of that breed. My dad used to sing and play 'That Strawberry Roan' and that got me wondering what a roan was. He tried to explain about the black legs and the different colors of the coat, but even he couldn't explain it so I understood fully."

"Well, all I really know is some that are called roans really aren't 'cause they don't carry the right genes."

"True roans should not carry two red genes, but instead should carry one or two non-red, which would be black. Confused yet?"

"Probably. All I really know is I know a blue roan when I see it. They're one of the prettiest horses on four legs."

She reined in. "Now *that* is an opinion, and therefore debatable."

He brought his mount to a halt. "Are we having our first argument?"

"Absolutely not. We're having an intelligent discussion in which one of us disagrees with the other without it coming to a shouting contest or worse violence."

"That sounds like something you read."

She laughed. "It is."

"Okay, I give. You've got four years of reading and studying on me while I was shooting Germans." Before she could say anything, he held up a hand. "That was unfair of me. Oh, wait—*look.*"

Mark put a finger to his lips and pointed.

Out in the middle distance, the yellow mare appeared like a ghost through a stand of gold-crowned cottonwoods. Her flanks shimmered in the evening sun, the same golden shade as the leaves on the trees around her.

Julie gasped. "Oh my God!"

The mare paid them no mind until Julie's gelding snorted. Across the way, the other horse raised her head, mane blowing in the breeze. For a moment, Mark didn't spot the colt, then saw her move delicately from behind her mother and mock the same head movement.

He could hardly breathe he was so taken by the beauty of the blue roan. He absolutely had to have that pair. Not today, of course, but soon. He would bring Jones out here with him. Together, they could cut the two out of the bunch and drive them into the corral.

His mind flashed back to the day he and Jones and Alma had captured those first six ponies on the ranch up in Bloody Basin. It was a breathtaking memory that made his heart thunder again in his chest. Some things were just too perfect to forget, and for a moment, it was as if Alma and Jones rode alongside him once again.

"I think they've seen us."

The stallion of the band—a tall, powerfully-built dun with a brown strip down his back—had, indeed, caught sight of them. He threw his head high and screamed. The herd turned and bolted, vanishing in a matter of moments, leaving nothing but a cloud of red dust swirling about in the last rays of the day.

"Baby, someday, we'll have that colt. I'll make him your wedding present." He reined his mount around and she followed him back to the ranch.

The air had turned colder, the wind switching so it raced down off the distant mountains and swept through the valley.

It was a day he wouldn't soon forget.

———

Mark and Julie married the week before Christmas, not making a big deal out of it because of her parents' feelings about them. When she walked the short distance to him at the altar, he covered his mouth to hide his grin. She wore a beautiful pale blue gown and a ring of white daisies on her head. When the gown hiked up a bit as she walked, her bare toes showed. Her smile was wider than he'd ever seen it when he slipped the ring on her finger. The only thing missing were her parents and he hated that for her sake. Everyone told them that Conroy would come around once grandbabies made an appearance. He hoped so.

Dirty Shirt Jones attended. Sam stood up with Mark and a friend of Julie's from U of A drove out to be her bridesmaid. All the cowboys from the farm at Lehi and the ranch in Paradise Valley came and shared cake and champagne with the newly-wed couple.

It was a fine day all around to Mark's way of thinking. He liked simple and Julie liked what he liked. Most of the time. She could present a strong argument when necessary, but mostly they didn't quarrel, and he liked that. It made for a peaceful existence.

The house wasn't finished, so he got one of the trailers fixed up to live in till it was. Neither wanted to wait any longer to be together. Julie said she didn't mind the trailer at all. After Christmas, besides work on the ranch, he would go back to rodeoing and so would she. It was a union made in heaven. If it weren't for Bryce Conroy's agitation.

12

THEY HONEYMOONED IN A MOTEL in Lehi for twenty-four hours
straight, but he worried about his stock at home, so they rode out to
the ranch. Everything was fine. Logs were going up on the house, but
he paced a lot, wanting it to go faster.

"Don't worry. I don't mind the trailer and we want it to be perfect."

He managed to stop his grumbling. They began the move of a few of her
things from Sonata and his from the bunkhouse.

By the weekend, they'd settled in the trailer and had her horse in his barn.

He stared into empty cabinets. Living alone, he'd settled for eating with the
hands in the bunkhouse, but it was time they bought food.

"We're out of groceries. We need to check on Rosita. She probably wonders
why we haven't stuck our noses out for so long. For some reason, there's no hot
water. Do you need to call your folks? I better call Sam in the morning."

"Calm down. You go check on Rosita. I can light the hot water heater and
I'll be all clean when you get back. You can bathe, and we'll go shopping for
food. How's that?"

"Fine." He chuckled. She could sure keep things in order.

Good damn thing.

He went down and leaned inside Rosita's door. "We're okay. When we go to town, can you clean up the trailer some and do the wash?"

She smiled. "I can remember when I first married my husband. We never slept. We never ate. It was so much fun. You and her are a good couple and have such a fine time."

He worried what she might think, him moving in with a woman, so he hurried to reassure her. "Rosita, you have a job here. Things won't ever be normal again, but we will all have fun and we appreciate you. Make me a list and I will get your things for you."

"I will do that. You are lucky to find her."

"She found me, but I'm happy."

Once they settled down together, lots of things became obvious. Julie was ranch-raised by parents who had everything. He was farm-raised by sharecroppers who had nothing. How alike could they be? Not much, even if people considered him rich and eccentric. She'd never picked cotton. Tall as she was, she'd have been bent over double getting to the bolls.

She was a CPA and he was an idiot. He loved her differently from how he loved Alma. He could never replace that first love, one that grew naturally from necessity. He'd never married the Pima Indian girl, never had the chance, but he would have, had the time come. None of it mattered. What did, and always would, is that he was head over heels for Julie. Didn't matter how different they were. It would work.

Back at the Arizona State Fair Grounds, he took the bucking stock off water. He started to separate the livestock for the last performance, horses first, and watched some head slinging Brahma bulls and a black cross who'd put a few guys in the hospital during his bucking career.

The bucking horses were easy. They'd been sorted before. The bulls took some time, but eventually they left the main arena. He had them cut off. He looked up and here she came on her big horse. Damn, she looked good.

"I was coming," she said. "Calves or steers?"

"Steers first. Then calves."

That pony of hers knew cattle and he soon had the dogging stuff separated. In the alleyway, he cut off the steers as she brought them to him. Then they penned the calves. She slipped off her horse and came over to him. He kissed her, *Life* Magazine style—wrapped in his arms, her legs long and slim. This time she laughed when he finished the kisses.

"You're a dandy, Mark Shaw." She dragged off her saddle. "Remember when we met, and you asked me in that way you have to tease me? 'What do you like to be called?' You didn't even know my name, did you?"

"No, ma'am."

"You thought you were so sly." She waved her finger at him. "I caught you."

"I give up." She'd never know it was the other way around. From the first moment he spied her, it was catch her or die from the need.

"What is my name? Julie Shaw. I'm married to that Mark Shaw. Plain as can be." She looked hard at him.

"Nothing plain about you."

She put her face on his shoulder. "That first night, you wanted to take me home with you, huh? Why didn't you? I never slept one bit thinking of you."

"I had the same problem. Waiting to do anything till we got hitched was kind of like giving up meat for Lent, wasn't it?"

"What did Rosita think about me? At first, I mean?"

"She is a dear sweet woman. She's a soldier's widow and I guess she never found anyone. She goes to mass every Sunday morning. But what brought all this up? We're legal and well married, so we can do as we please."

"Just some things with us have been... well, different than I expected, that's all. I'm still trying to figure how I fit into your life and my relationship with the other people there."

"Julie, you're my wife. Sure, I have a lot of other people in my life, friends, business associates, bankers, lawyers, Hollywood folks, but none of them are as important to me as you. Does that answer your question?"

"Thank you. I guess that's what I needed to hear," she said, kissing him on the cheek just as the door opened.

Pamela brought him the list of stock drawn by the judges. He thanked her. She spoke politely to Julie and Julie said she always did a good job.

The secretary grinned. "Of course. Mark hires good sorting help." She headed back inside.

"I pay them so much."

She and Julie laughed at his joke.

They soon had the numbers sorted and went for a hamburger from a vendor already open.

When the guy gave them the burgers and fries, they carried them up to sit on the rodeo bleachers. "At least no baloney sandwiches tonight."

"I'd eat them with you. Even in the backseat."

"Sure, now that you've got me lassoed good and proper."

He held up the thick hamburger. "No, I ate baloney all my life. We used it for bacon in the morning. Then for lunch with mustard on biscuits and in spaghetti at supper. And we was damn lucky to have that too."

"Well, you've come a long way now."

He winked. "I sure have. Got me this purty rodeoing woman and everything is just dandy." They both laughed. He was laughing a lot lately and it felt good.

"We ate a lot better up on the ranch," he said. "But hell, over across the water we ate C rations and baloney would have tasted damn good."

"You're like Daddy. He eats potatoes and beef and then beef and potatoes."

"A man after my own heart." If only that were actually true. Would he and Bryce ever be friends?

She doused French fries in ketchup and ate them one by one, her pinky finger crooked just so. "Oh, more shades of home. Tell me about your best horse."

"That's a long story. I came home hearing artillery and machine guns in my head, seeing all my buddies who didn't make it. I wanted to get on a horse and ride, ride, ride. Just ride away. My stepmother, Lenora, wanted me to go see a *bruja*. She meant well. Instead, Dirty Shirt Jones and I, along with Alma, went off to catch some bachelor wild horses in the McDowell Mountains.

"It took us two weeks, but we caught five. Sold one for a stallion, the rest we gelded. I caught my great sorrel horse and we broke him riding up into Bloody Basin. There was no road left into the ranch back then, it had washed out." He paused to take a great bite of the burger and chew it. Staring off into space. Thinking.

She filled the silence. "Wow, I've heard some of that story. But it's good hearing more. There were lots of unbranded cattle?"

"We culled cattle for three months, six truckloads a week. Sam and I made a fortune. That's how I have the ranch now in Paradise Valley. He bribed me to sell out the place at Bloody Basin with this place. I guessed I'd never have sold the ranch otherwise."

"This ranch is perfect—or will be. Are you sorry you sold the other one?"

"Nope. Not at all. It's all worked out well. And here, you and I are doing the thing we love best to do." She popped a grin. "Well, maybe the second best."

They were both quiet for a while. How much should he share with her? He didn't want her to think too badly of his family. His dad had done the best he could under the circumstances.

"Tell me some more. I like hearing you talk about life then."

He swallowed then went on. "We lost Grandpa's ranch up at Congress back then. I cried for months over that deal as a young boy. We were sharecroppers then. My mom, dad, and I hoed cotton, then we picked cotton. I *hate* cotton."

"I can tell you do. I don't blame you."

"You better get dressed for the rodeo, babe. I have a feeling about tonight. You may win that queen contest tonight."

"If I do, will you come in the arena and swing me around like you did Linda?"

"Damn right, I will if you want me to. Only difference is you got britches on and her bare legs were kicking high. How will I get a picture? Oh, I know. Clarence, the rodeo photographer. He'll make me an eight-by-ten."

She frowned at him in disbelief. "Not sure my daddy would like that. But we're married now, so it's too bad if he doesn't. Are you serious? What if I don't win?"

"Even if you don't win, I'll be down there just as if you did. Bail off that horse and I'll kiss you and he'll get our picture. But you know, it will be on the front page of the *Arizona Republic* on Sunday. Cowboy does it again."

They about died laughing. She hurried off to change. He went to find Clarence. The photographer agreed instantly, excited to be let in on their deal.

Lonnie found him before grand entry. "I saw you with that queen. Heard you married her at Christmas. You two looked very serious eating together."

"Well, we are very serious. A fella don't get married if he ain't." There he went again, laughing.

Lonnie slapped his leg. "You are the luckiest bastard I know. First you find an abandoned ranch, you make a movie set out of it, you hit an artesian well, and you're richer than anyone I know. Bankers stand up when you come in the room. And now you've gone and married a rodeo queen."

"Well, now I have a wife. But things will be the same with the rodeo. She loves it and will come along."

Lonnie looked pleased. "I have the Tucson rodeo next month. Will you help me out there?"

"Sure."

"At least I won't have to look at your ugly face all the time. I can look at her."

Lonnie went off and Mark went to help line up the grand entry in the alleyway. Working these big rodeos was fun. Maybe he'd try his hand at doing it more someday. Julie would like that.

Soon they struck up the band and the American flag came in first. Everyone stood, and he swept off his hat—yes, God bless America and he was ready to kiss the ground that he stood upon, horseshit and all.

He waved when she swept by him in line with all the rest. Ladies first, barrel racers in glittering shirts and white hats, cowboys all done up in their finest, clowns walking along behind. A restored stagecoach pulled by six prancing quarter horses, the driver waving. Tonight, he had some fun planned.

After bareback broncs, the queens were introduced one by one, each accompanied by a drum roll.

The announcer called out Miss Congeniality. Julie won best in speech, then Horsemanship—Julie won second, but he rated her first. Finally, he called out again, *"The winner of Miss Arizona Rodeo is from Sonata, Arizona."*

She threw her white-gloved free hand to the middle of her chest.

"Ladies and gentlemen, here she is! Our new queen, Julie Conroy Shaw."

She rode over to the center. Clarence flashed his camera and they crowned her.

"Julie, make a victory pass, and lead these girls out. Here she goes." The voice boomed over the crowd's cheering, and she rounded the arena riding high. On the way out, she waved the girls by her, put a reining skid on her horse, piled off and Mark ran to kiss her. They were greeted with a huge cheer from the crowd, so loud it could've been heard back home.

When he swept her up, the announcer spoke into the mic. *"Ladies and gentleman, you know this man. A few years ago, he made the* Life *magazine cover with another lady. He's a stock contractor, too. Name is Mark Shaw and there is lots to tell you about him. He's a highly-decorated war hero and he can sure pick a pretty woman to kiss, as well."* He paused, glanced at a note someone handed him. *"Oh, here's the best part! Miss Julie Conroy married Mark Shaw last Christmas. So, give them another big hurrah!"*

To the roar and whistling of the crowd, Mark led her by the hand to the open gate. A pickup man brought her horse. He tossed the reins to Mark. Then they confronted two people—a tall cowboy in a tailored western suit, and a pretty woman beside him who looked like her daughter, but not as tall.

Bryce and Eleanor Conroy.

Mark swelled with pride. At last, he'd impressed the stubborn S-O-B. enough to earn his presence. A firm handshake from her dad, a hug from mom. Had he at last measured up to her family, or were they just making a show? Conroy's eyes gleamed and Eleanor looked happy. Their acceptance of him as their son-in-law was real.

One more victory.

"It may not be on *Life,*" her daddy said, shaking his head. "But you two will make the Sunday edition for sure."

At that, she hugged Mark, almost jumping up and down. "You got it done for me, baby!"

"Wasn't nothing that I won't take a hundred razzings for, over and over again. But I reckon it was worth it, all in all." With her, he wasn't going to live a life as it ever was before. But he wasn't a bit worried about that. Whatever came, he would enjoy it.

They took a load of stock home that evening. He would come back in the morning for the rest. She hauled her horse and, once at the ranch, put him in a stall. The stock unloaded, they went toward the trailer.

Rosita came out on the porch built on her trailer. "I left the lights on, 'cause I knew you were coming home tonight."

"I'll turn it off later. Thanks."

Inside his trailer, she hugged him. "How do I take care of you?"

"Just be here with me." He rocked her with them standing in the middle of the living room. The lights dimmed every so often with a dip in the voltage, but the generator rolled on.

"I can see where I'm going. Back to the Salt River Power authority and get some poles set coming out here."

"Oh, Mark, I could just sit in candlelight with you."

"Light some. I'll go shut the dang thing off."

"Don't be gone long."

About then, out in one of the pastures, a coyote let out a deep call. "Don't be afraid. They're just happy for us."

"I'm not. They've howled all my life on our ranch."

"Good, we have a big crop of them out here."

He went to turn off the generator. They slept together in each other's arms. At daylight, she woke him with a kiss, then fled the bed.

He stood in the door in jeans and a flannel shirt. She was having a time getting used to the small kitchen.

"Better than eating someone else's cooking all the time, isn't it?"

"Oh, yeah?" She tossed the words over her shoulder. "We'll take turns cooking just like we take turns breaking horses and shoveling horse droppings."

"That'll be the day."

Dressed in one of his long-tailed shirts for a nightie, she kept right on frying bacon and eggs. Toast popped up and she still hadn't had a comeback. Had he made her mad?

He didn't say anything about the coffee, one tablespoon short, for fear it would fluff her feathers.

"Didn't act much like newlyweds last night. Sorry about that. I was worn out."

"Me, too. Guess we're just an old married couple, huh?"

He hugged her while she cleaned the table off. "That'll never happen, my love. I'm rested if you are."

She put down the dish cloth, took his hand, and led him to the back of the trailer where they slept, kissing him. "We'll always be together, I promise."

Having lost Alma, the promise went straight to his soul. No one could make that kind of promise, but he took it anyway, tucking it up against his heart. He hoped to God she was right about that. He knew what it was like to lose the one you loved and how lucky he was to have been given this second chance.

Later that morning, after washing the dishes, they loaded her horse. She headed to Tempe and he went to the fairgrounds to load up his stock.

13

MARK NEVER FELT CERTAIN ABOUT leaving his own life and moving into theirs, but Julie took over his bookkeeping and organization. Not too bossy, but simply organizing everything. He had a calendar for where he needed to be and when, and in some cases why. In a month, she had all of their money lying around in interest-paying accounts.

They were seated at the chrome-vinyl kitchen table and looking at house plans for the ranch. As the builder put it, the house was closed in. The logs and roof were done. From the outside, it was beautiful. Inside, an upper balcony overlooking the downstairs would lead to six bedrooms and baths. The downstairs layout was still under consideration. The master bedroom on the main floor would have floor-to-ceiling glass windows, and French doors leading out to the patio and pool. That was a given. It was just the rest of it that remained in the discussion stage.

"Do you really think we can get electric out here?"

"Yep. I just haven't tried hard enough. Sam is working on it."

She reached over and squeezed his forearm. "That would be nice. When can we go see the movie ranch?"

"How about tomorrow? We can load Red and another horse for you in your trailer and head out up there. We'll need to use your rig. My old International would never pull them in there."

"Can't I take Thunder?" She looked disappointed.

"Hey, that country is rough up there. Let's leave him here for the smooth stuff."

"I suppose you're right."

"What are we going to do today?"

Her face lit up. "What do you say? Honeymoon it?"

"That's the word. Let me check the livestock and everything. I'll be right back."

"Drink your coffee first. I want to take you down to Sonata in the next week."

"We can go." He finished his coffee and put on a lined jumper.

He stepped out the door and was glad he pulled on the jumper. It was cold outside, and he hunched up against the wind. Rosita came out in a long coat.

He stopped and smiled. "How are you doing?"

"Fine. Do you need anything?"

He glanced back at their trailer. "Not today. Tomorrow we'll take off."

She laughed. "I'll clean the house then."

With a light hug from him, she went back inside.

The rodeo cattle were fine, eating green alfalfa hay, with their water tank full. The horses in the pen were okay, so he fed her horse and Red in the stalls. He checked the azure sky. Must be forty degrees with a northern wind. They had some frost earlier in the week but in a day or so, it would be warm enough to show her the movie ranch. All he dreaded was that damn son of the guy who bought it. Maybe he'd be off somewhere bragging about his money.

Chores done, he went back to the house after checking the diesel supplies at the chugging generator. He'd need Sam's help to get the power line strung. His partner could do anything like that. Satisfied, he headed back for the trailer. Having her was like having Alma. They weren't to be compared, but they both pleased him and, better yet, they liked the role.

Would it wear off? He hoped not. He warmed up in front of the butane stove in the living room.

Then she came out in a white robe and smiled. "Took you long enough."

He laughed, and bear hugged her. "I was running the whole time."

Her long hair hung loose, and she let it fall over one eye like Veronica Lake. "I would have waited if you took four hours, Big Boy."

Laughing, she led him back to the first bedroom.

——

THEY WENT TO SEE SAM the very next day. The ranch trip was postponed for a while, and Sam called up the Salt River Power Authority to speak to Eldon Carpenter, the top man. Mark and Julie sat in leather chairs facing the desk. When Sam leaned back in his chair and put his feet up, Mark knew to settl in for a long, persuasive talk.

"Damnit, Eldon, we need power for a decorated hero. He's out there making a paradise out of the valley by the same name. He's got eighty acres of alfalfa and is going to build a movie set out there. You can't hold back progress. We need juice out there. I know everyone needs to be hooked up, but you won't lose a cent on this deal. That's right." Sam held his hand over the mouthpiece. "We're going to get it. You kids go have fun. Before sunset, I'll have power headed that way."

They waved goodbye and went out the office door. In the Chevy pickup, they drove out to Superstition Mountain to check on things at the movie set. The false front buildings were about up, and the place looked great. A crew of Mexicans from Gilbert were building corrals to hold the horses and teams that they'd need for filming. He spoke to Salazar, the man who ran the crew.

"We should finish here this week."

"Good, we can build a few more out at my place the following week."

"Oh, sure. We can be there. How big?"

"I'll have the plans drawn up and the lumber on the site."

They shook hands and he went back to Julie, who was talking to the man who was the overseer—a small balding fellow with a comb-over that stood in the air in the wind. He didn't seem to notice. Julie did and was doing her best not to laugh. Her struggle amused him as much as the man's. The longer they lived together, the more he enjoyed himself.

"That bunch from Hollywood was here. I was telling her. They came out here in a jeep and that director got out holding his back. It was funny. He kicked the tires, swearing about why they drove that stiff riding thing from the hotel out there when the roads were all paved."

"Sounds like everything is going to plan." Mark covered his mouth with a doubled fist and made a coughing sound.

They had barely moved out of the overseer's sight before they both busted out laughing.

"Looks like he could use some glue." Mark held open the pickup's door for her. "Guess I shouldn't laugh. One of these days, I might lose all my hair. Then what would I do?"

"Oh, you'd be just as handsome bald as you are now." She patted his head. "Well, maybe not quite. You might need to order you some glue."

"Yeah, thanks. It looks like everything's going according to schedule. Reckon we can go back home. Funny how they can put up store fronts and make the place look so real when there's nothing behind the walls."

"It is a fascinating business."

"Yes, but when I was in that one movie, they spent forever getting a scene on film. Guess in a way it's okay. The stars get a lot of down time to contemplate the meaning of life."

She punched him easy-like on the arm. "Meaning of life? You're getting plumb philosophical."

They drove back home, calling Sam from a phone booth in a bar.

He listened to the good news. *"No problem, sonny boy. Hire an electrician and get everything set. He's sending three crews out after they survey it tomorrow. Son, I wish you'd get a telephone out there, so I could call you once in a while."*

"Well, I would. All you have to do is wrangle me one of them too. Can't they use the same poles? Tell 'em to string me some wire for a phone while they're at it.'

"Oh, just like that?"

"In my opinion, what Sam Cline wants, he gets. Just like that."

"Oh, is that right? I thought you might say that, so I went ahead and ordered the lines and phones for both your living quarters and your office."

"Well, thanks pard, we'll be ready."

Back in the pickup, he grinned at her.

"Did he do it?"

She sounded excited. Wait till she heard the rest.

"Ol' Sambo came through. Not only that, we're getting phones, too."

She clapped her hands to both cheeks and let out a low squeal. He hugged her and started the truck. "They will be there in a week with juice. Might take a little longer to get the telephones put in."

They drove home listening to country music on the new radio station up in Glendale. That was all they played—country music. Some well-known DJ named Ray Odum built it with all the money he made the past August from a packed Elvis Presley concert at the fairgrounds. They went on home and celebrated.

The next morning, Mark was in Sam's office. The movie producer, Zack Holder, who talked like Elmer Fudd in the Bugs Bunny cartoons, wanted changes on the Superstition set. They always wanted changes, but the deal was the set was built to their specs where they drove stakes. So, any great change was going to cost the producer and he was upset.

In the room full of lawyers and people, including Mark, Sam finally said, "These are your plans. What do you want to change Mister Holder?"

"We need an asphalt runway to wand airpwanes."

Sam winced. "You're shooting a western, not a war movie. Why in the he—I mean where will that be a part of the script?"

The lawyer, Sam Goldstein, quickly replied, his thick mustache wiggling up and down. "Our contract with the star requires—"

"Did we sign that one?" Sam asked in disbelief and his lawyer from Phoenix, who was so good looking he could've been in movies, shook his head.

"No, sir."

"Good," Sam said, leaning back. "An asphalt landing strip long enough for a two-engine private plane costs forty thousand dollars. I have three bids right here from airport contractors. The time they need to build it is nine months. The liability insurance for owning one is a policy that costs two thousand dollars a year if there are no wrecks out there. The contract for the movie set for nine months increases at three thousand dollars a month according to your contract. Now, Mister Holder, what do you wish to do?"

There was lot of whispering among lawyers and movie officials. Mark heard a portion of it.

Sounded to him like they would need to buy out the actor.

Holder rose. "Can we adjourn for thwee days?"

"Adjourn for whatever," Sam said. "Your lease is signed, and the cost goes on."

"Thank you." Everyone shook hands. The movie people left, and all were frowning like the next strike was the bombing of Mesa, Arizona. He heard part of another comment going out, mentioning, "—these hicks."

When the office was clear, the three gathered back at the coffee table. "Dear God, that was tewible." Mark burst out laughing at Sam's mockery.

When they all quieted down, Sam asked Mark if the meeting had gone to suit him and folded his hands on the polished table top.

"All but one thing. Those wool suit bastards referring to us as hicks."

Their lawyer, Paul Thompson, laughed and Sam did too. Then he continued, "Who was dumb enough to sign a contract that required an asphalt runway, anyway?"

"Paul, what will they do next?" Mark asked. "For that much money I can take being called a hick. Guess it's no worse than laughing at the way a man talks. But I just couldn't help it."

"Me either." Thompson tapped on the table with a pen. "I imagine they'll try to get out of it. They could even pay you the entire thirty thousand in their contract. But we could sue them for breach of contract and put a value on their nonuse, hurting our business by not using it."

"How much would that be?" Sam asked.

"Triple damages."

"I like that. What are our chances of winning that?"

"With a trial here in Maricopa County? Great. Who loves movie companies?"

Sam stretched and peered out at Main Street through the venetian blinds. "Partner, how is Julie?"

"Doing fine. When I left, she was running barrels on Thunder. We bought a Three-Bar colt. He needs lots of training, but he runs like Man of War."

"She's not made any plans to leave you, has she?"

Mark chuckled. "Not before I left out there."

"The Ford dealer is getting in a dark blue Lincoln convertible next week. You want it as a present for her?"

"Why, Sam, they have a list a mile long—"

"I only asked if you wanted it."

"Sure, but we won't get it."

"The hell we won't. I'm on the head of that list and I can accept or refuse every new car that comes in."

Mark swallowed. What did that place cost him? "It sure don't hurt to have influential friends, does it? Yes, of course I'd like Julie to have that Lincoln. How much is it? I'll get you a check."

"No. It's a company car, but she will have possession of it. That way, if she ever gets mad at you, I can call in the car. These new cars are getting lots looser."

"I hope she never gets that mad, but I'm sure she'll drive it. When will it be here?"

"Next week. Cleaned up, seat covers changed to real leather with tuck and roll. Oh, give them two weeks. They will want folks to drool over it a few days in the showroom."

Mark smiled. "Let me know when it gets there. I'll take her by and show her. Don't let a word out."

They shook Paul's hand and thanked him. The lawyer looked Mark up and down. "You still ride wild horses?"

"Bucking horses? Yes, I do. I won a silver belt buckle down at Chandler two weeks ago."

"He's about to get electricity out to his place too," Sam said. "Then we need a phone line strung out there, so I can call him."

"My, I'd love to see your place." Paul fastened his briefcase.

"Not much out there now, but in another few months we'll have our new house finished. All but the pool, and it'll take a few more. Then I'll throw a party."

"Save me an invite."

"Me, too," Sam said.

Mark aimed a pistol finger at them. "You two'll be the first ones that I invite."

"Maybe we should have a blowout for her car at my house," Sam said, squeezing his chin. "Can I do that, Mark?"

"Hell, yes."

"I sure like dealing with hicks." Paul sounded amused. "They feed me so good."

Mark left Sam's office, picked up some things his wife and Rosita wanted, filled the car with gas at a Shell station, then headed home for Scottsdale and up the dusty road out into Paradise Valley. Past Camelback Mountain, he turned off on the yet-unnamed section line road that went out to his place.

Driving along beside the road in the mesquite, he must have spooked the big golden mare. Running along side her was the blue roan colt.

Damn they were pretty, free and running hard. It was time he and Jones got out there and ran them down.

There were reward posters for the both. He wasn't sure who offered the reward and he didn't care anything about it. How it had gotten started that they were out there he had no idea. But idiots were racing around all over the country after them. They were so spooked getting even close would be a chore.

Running like that right next to him was like God saying here's your chance, but you'd better hurry, before someone else gets 'em. It reminded him how bad he wanted that blue roan, but he was getting too busy to think about doing it.

He eased off the gas pedal and the mare swung north into the saguaros, mesquite, greasewood, and bunch grass. Soon she was gone, the colt keeping up with her easily.

A true blue roan horse—or colt in this instance—was worth a lot, but it wasn't the money he cared about. It was the rarity and beauty of it. There were several roans, but a blue was what one rarely saw. Take a strawberry roan or the black, which some folks tried to pawn off as a blue, and several other shades and colors which were pretty common. Giving Julie that blue roan colt would be far more than the equivalent of that fancy blue Lincoln. But he'd give her both in more than a heartbeat, he thought that much of her. Nothing would be worth what he felt for the beautiful woman. He'd never believed he could love anyone like he loved her.

Damn. All that reward did was make her wilder. Every drugstore cowboy had been out there chasing her. They didn't know shit about catching wild horses. All they did was make her foxier than she would have been left alone.

Some maverick-chasing cowboys the ex-corporate giant hired tried for three weeks to trap her and no telling what they charged the man. But catching unbranded bovines was a damn sight easier than rounding up wild horses, especially the smart ones. He sat in the car seat and his mouth watered. What was he waiting for? He should've gone out the first time he spotted them, but so dang much was going on. The time was here.

Julie would be with him on this, he was certain. What was Dirty Shirt doing those days? They needed to go visit him and see what he thought about catching a red dun mare and her six-month-old blue roan colt.

A brainstorm set in. What would a Hollywood producer give for the footage of the chase to later be spliced into a movie? The star could be added like he was in on the deal later.

Damn, he was getting like Sam. Been around him too much. He put the pickup back in gear. Judging by the sun, it was damn near lunchtime.

When he pulled up to the ranch, a flatbed ton-and-half Chevy farm truck sat in front of his house. Danged if he didn't see his dad with his butt against the fender under a straw hat and wearing khakis roll himself a cigarette, light it, and let loose a mouth full of smoke. Dad only smoked when under pressure. He recalled how he went to smoking when his mom was in the Phoenix Hospital before she died.

He parked beside him. "What do you say, Dad?"

"Cotton may be a dollar a pound, but these farmers have six-row equipment now and need less farm help. I was told this was my last year two weeks ago. Oh, we can stay down there this year, we've got the ground ready to plant cotton when it gets warm enough. I could go work for the International dealer in Chandler, but I wondered if you had work out here."

"I've got eighty acres of alfalfa, rodeo stock to haul and feed. I do some cattle hauling. What does he pay you?" Anxious to help out his father, Mark right quick mentally tallied a wage.

"Two fifty a month."

That wouldn't be hard to meet or beat. "I have a new partner. I need to talk to her. Come to the house and meet her. We got married at Christmas. Just small, didn't invite anyone. Sorry I hadn't been down since then. Let's go in and talk to her about this deal."

"That's great, son. Congratulations. Say, I didn't come in here to beg on you—"

"Hell, no. I need you." He moved in and hugged his shoulder. "Did you tell her who you were?" He nodded toward the trailer.

Dad shook his head. "I didn't want to bother her."

Mark held the screen door open for his dad and followed him inside. Something smelled mighty good. That sweet wife of his was cooking up a good meal.

"Darling, this is my father, Carl. You ain't met yet. Dad, this is Julie."

She rushed over and hugged each man in turn. "Why didn't you say so, instead of waiting outside?"

"He didn't want to bother you. I told him you weren't easily bothered."

"Heavens no. Well, don't ever do it again." She wrinkled her nose. "I'll forgive you this time. It's almost lunchtime. Can I feed you both?"

"Sure. The way it smells, I'll just bet you could." Mark let his grin move from her to Dad. The old man nodded, looking pleased. He wished he'd been better about visiting them.

"Have a seat. I won't be long. How did the meeting go this morning?"

"Sam stood our ground. They left mumbling about dealing with hicks."

"Hicks?" Her face showed disbelief.

Dad looked puzzled but didn't ask anything.

"Yeah, hicks. Made me mad, but our lawyer Paul said we'd sue them for triple damages if they messed with us anymore. Then they might refrain from calling us that."

Everyone laughed.

She grilled them some strip steaks in the broiler oven, German fried potatoes with sweet onions, and some baking powder biscuits that had already been in the oven when they came in. They talked some about his father's future. Julie was immediately enthusiastic about the family moving onto their ranch, even talked about building them something to live in.

"I guess the school bus would come out here." Mark buttered his last biscuit.

"It comes way up Scottsdale Road. Oh, they would." She looked at his dad. "Did you see we have electricity coming?"

"Well, you have the poles, anyway."

"No, Sam talked to the main man. We are priority." Then she laughed. "Way back yonder, Mark said you and Sam had words?"

"We almost had a fight. I about quit, but finished out the year on his place. Sam wanted me to stop cultivating the cotton way too soon and we'd spent all summer hoeing weeds, so he could save a few gallons of gas."

Mark chuckled. "I always wondered what all that was about. Now I know."

His dad shook his head. "He wanted me to stop using the tractor to cultivate and put you and your mother and me out there hoeing all summer in that heat. We weren't a big family like some of his farmers. Her health wasn't that good by then, either."

"I always wondered about that." Hard to believe about Sam, but business was business, at least with Sam.

"He bought the fuel and asked me to stay. But I had all I wanted of him."

Julie served them some apple pie. "Don't get me in any cotton hoeing projects, Mark Shaw. If I can't do it from a horse, forget about me."

"Son—" he used his fork to point at his pie "—this woman fixes some mighty good groceries on her table. I wouldn't make her too mad."

Mark winked at her. "I'll try not to do that."

After hugs and kisses and more talk about hiring him, Carl headed for home. She sent along a few frozen packages of meat from their locker that was in her new chest freezer.

"Lenore will love you."

"I want to see all his brothers and sister too. She's the baby, isn't she?"

"Yeah, and growing fast. Come any time. We may have beans cooked, but we can feed you two." Then he kissed her on the cheek and Mark took him to his truck.

When Mark came back in the house, he said, "Next time you see him, he won't be smoking."

"Why?"

"He only smokes when something upsets him."

"And coming here upset him? That's too bad." She was in his arms kissing him. "We'll fix them a house and job out here, won't we?"

"Yes. You bet we'll do that." He rubbed her back. "I saw that red dun mare and her blue roan colt today. I want them, and I know you do too after laying eyes on them."

"We need to do something about catching them. I want to be in on the chase."

"I'm not a bit surprised. Bet your bottom dollar you will be. So now all we need to do is round up a claybank mare and her blue roan colt. It hadn't ought to be too hard with the three of us experts going after them."

She squeezed his face and kissed him, as excited as he was.

They had horses to catch was his last thought before going to sleep much later that night.

14

MARK LOOKED AT A FORDILLAC at the dealership. Since cotton prices soared so high, many ranchers had bought Ford pickups, removed the engine and transmission, and dropped in a Cadillac V8 with a hydromatic transmission. They damn sure would pull her double horse trailer over the mountains.

The salesman said he could sell it to him for fifteen hundred. The light green truck had less than seven thousand miles on the speedometer. He bought it for delivery to the house after they had it cleaned up and added new custom leather seats in it.

Word was, they really were working on the Black Canyon Highway to Prescott. A super highway that eventually would go to Flag. It would be a much easier and faster way to go to the movie ranch. They'd pull their horses up there with his new purchase.

Mark had two meetings at Sam's office with some serious moviemakers who were making a new series. He wasn't sure they didn't want partners to get the job done. Julie had gone shopping and had several bags from local downtown stores around her chair in the lobby when they came out.

"Saturday night at my house we are having a big western parry for some movie folks." Sam squeezed her hands then hugged her. "You can come and be my hostess."

"Wild horses couldn't drag me away."

"Now that is big talk. I know you love horses."

"You are on that same list. Did he tell you he bought a new toy? One of those Cadillac pickups to haul my horses."

"No." Sam slanted a look at Mark. Grinned. "That rascal, you'll like that, all right."

"What time is the party?"

"Oh, come early and be my hostess. Dress western."

"What's the menu?"

"Mesquite grilled steaks and all the trimmings. I have a Texas Swing band coming, too."

"Sounds great."

Mark took her to meet John in Scottsdale to go over his house plans. They were going to Los Olivos Restaurant for the best Mexican food in town and *quesadillas,* too.

"Those men you met today real?" She picked at a thread on her skirt.

"Yes, one is a real actor, Don Red Berry. They want to make a pilot for a new series."

"I couldn't recall his name. But I knew he was an actor when they came out. What does Sam think?"

"They're looking for money."

She smiled, and he parked at the restaurant. They had reserved a large table and John had the plans spread out, rooms drawn for both floors.

A waiter in red pants and a white blousy shirt took their drink order. Mark wanted to talk about the mare and her colt, but this was about the house. Wine arrived and a tall glass of tea for Mark along with a big platter of *quesadillas* for appetizers. Julie sipped red wine and nibbled from a wedge of the *quesadilla* made from large flour tortillas sandwiched around melted cheese.

She stopped beside Mark. "I know we could afford that *hacienda* style house, and it was beautiful. But the log ranch we settled on is beautiful. It's more us."

Mark studied the room plans John had laid out. Why was she still asking about the *hacienda?* The log structure was built. Designing the inner rooms was what this was about. Maybe she was having second thoughts. Lord, he hoped not. Women were that way sometimes. He tapped the huge master bedroom. "Closets, one for each of us so she can buy all the clothes she wants."

John chuckled. "Yes, here. And a bath for two. Two of everything except the jacuzzi, but it's big enough for two."

"Is this what you want?" He took her hand, lying on the table.

"Of course, but you?"

"I am *not* the woman of the house."

"No, but you *are* the man. We can have hitch rails out in front. Still have a great patio to entertain in back and a pool. The large beams across the living areas and hardwood floors are going to be wonderful. I want to pick the light fixtures. And we can cool what part we want to use. It is big."

"Is that all that worries you?" John leaned back and sighed.

Poor man. Mark laid his hand over hers. "It's beautiful the way it is. We like it big. Yes?" He nodded toward Julie.

"Yes. Only change I would like to make is a larger pantry off the kitchen and take the size from the kitchen space. Rosita should not have to walk so far from range, to fridge, to sink."

The waiter returned to take their order and John rolled up the plans, looking pleased. "No more changes once we begin the rooms. You can choose paint colors. Agreed?"

"Yes. This style is us, I agree."

He drank Coke, John drank beer, and she drank red wine. They spent over an hour visiting and talking about the house, but it was settled at last. The matter did make Mark a lot more comfortable. John said it was their house and needed to be like they wanted it.

Slouched in the captain's chair, Mark enjoyed his steak while his mind wandered to the mare and her colt. John enjoyed his meal, chatting with Julie about getting someone to put in the pool. Listening to Julie's lilting voice, he imagined her in something skimpy, jumping into crystal clear water and coming up laughing. The Lincoln convertible would surprise and please her. Sam wanted to spoil her, too.

"Feel better now?" She drove them back home.

"Hey, I would have lived in a tent with you, but I love the plans. A real ranch house. You know I was raised in an adobe shack on some crop farm around here. I spent summers up at Congress at Grandfather's ranch till he lost it. This will be my first real home. To have it with you, pleases me."

"I talked to Mom. She wishes we'd come down there and visit."

"Can they wait till we catch that mare and colt?"

She broke into laughter. "You talk about Sam and all his deals. Mark Shaw, you are as business-minded as he is."

"I told Jones we'd be up first thing as soon as we finished the deal on the house."

"All right. Let's go catch the horses first."

Mark frowned at all the pickups with racks and aluminum painted horse trailers parked all along the road while they headed down the section line going toward their place. Those damn amateur horse chasers were only making the mare wilder. None of them would ever catch her.

He wanted that blue roan colt about as bad as he'd wanted Julie. Not quite, but almost.

Boy, he wanted a lot.

———

JONES WAS SLEEPING IN A hammock in the warm afternoon sun when Mark came across the yard. Jones sat up, put on his unblocked hat, and looked hard at the pickup. "Why didn't she come with you?"

"She's afraid of real Indians."

"Oh, hell, I doubt that. We met at the wedding and she did not appear afraid. What has changed? Have you been telling her wild tales about our adventures?"

"Well, maybe. You ever get a woman?"

"Yeah."

"She here?"

"I guess, if she didn't run off."

"I'll get mine. You get yours. Why, we may even have a stomp here today."

Jones went rambling off to get his woman and Mark went back for Julie. They met at the hammock. Her name was Lupe. She was younger than Julie and wore a faded dress, with her dark hair in braids. They sat in green steel lawn chairs and Jones asked Julie where she grew up.

"I used to live in Tempe. I finished college and moved out to the ranch. My folks have a ranch at Sonata."

"He got electricity out to your place yet?"

"Oh, yes, a week ago we shut the generator off for good."

He made a face. "They won't ever get electricity up where he took me a few years ago. Man, we had to ride horses for three days to find it. It had no road."

"I wonder why he didn't keep it."

He shook his head. "Your crazy man would never have sold it, but Sam gave him that valley land or he'd still be up there."

"It didn't treat you so bad. You got this farm out of the deal." Mark turned to Lupe. "He was living in a *jacal* over in Lehi, Lupe. Not nice, like this place."

Lupe smiled. "I really like this place. I saw that one and I would have stayed at Sells before I would have gone up there to that."

"She has been to school," Jones said. "She can read and write and cooks good too. I was lucky to find her."

"Jones, I've got a deal for us. There is a red dun mare and her colt loose—"

"I know all about them. A man, name of Harry Price, came here one day and wanted me to go get them. Talked to me in sign language, like I didn't speak English. He kept asking if I would go catch them, like in the movies."

"What did you tell this Price?"

"He kept saying, 'I will pay you well. Will you do this for me?' I got so tired of him talking to me like that, I said, 'Fuck you and that mare and her colt. And fuck you for treating me like I was a second-class dumb Indian. Now get the fuck off my place.'"

By then, Jones was waving his arms and Mark and Julie were bent over in stitches. Lupe was giggling and finally managed to say, "He ran him off. That man actually ran to his station wagon, like he was going to scalp him, and roared away."

"Will you come help me?" Mark pointed and signed at Jones.

They laughed some more.

Finally, Jones managed to speak. "All those reward getters have done is get her more spooked. But Lupe can ride good. That would make four of us."

"Julie can ride, and I have enough horses shod and ready."

Jones nodded toward Mark and spoke to Julie. "He came in army clothes to my house wagon with an Indian girl I knew. He ever tell you that story?"

She shook her head.

So, Jones told her how they'd met and worked together on the Bloody Basin ranch and about Alma, too. When he finished talking about Alma's funeral, they were all in tears.

He took her hands and looked into her eyes. "I am so glad you're going to help him."

Lupe took the handkerchief from Mark and dried the tears from Jones's face.

"He told me many times that he appreciated her and you so much." Julie sniffed and wiped her eyes.

Jones stood. "Well, when do we ride?"

"Thursday?" Mark came away from staring out the window.

"Good."

"Come to our house the night before."

"No, she has chickens and the horses to see about." Jones shook his head.

Mark glanced at Lupe. "Can I hire someone to care for them?"

Jones looked at her. "Would your sister come?"

"I think so."

"We don't live fancy, Lupe. We have a trailer house. *Used.*" Julie accented the last word.

Lupe laughed.

With all things settled, Mark and Julie hurried off for home, grabbing their rural delivery mail out of the box.

"Will you go look for her with them?" she asked.

"Of course, but not without you."

"Great. I want to ride with you. Have you ever seen Jones cry before?"

"No, I never have seen any emotion from him. I guess her death was hard on him too. They chewed on each other all the time. Alma wanted him to find a wife. He said they cost too much. But after my Alma died he went and found Lupe, didn't he?"

She agreed. "Oh, Mark he's such a complex man."

"I think he's a great person. He damn sure told that guy who owns them horses to get out."

"But he was talking down to him like some guy in a bad movie." She shook her head.

"Chasing those horses will be fun."

"Yes, thanks for letting me go along."

"Hey, why did you think I wouldn't take you along?"

"I felt like I might be invading your world too much."

He stopped the car and turned to her. "Julie, you're my life."

They kissed for a while, then in a cloud of dust rushed home.

Later, they watched the snowy black and white TV news and he read the mail.

"Don't forget Sam's party Saturday night, baby. He asked you to be his hostess, remember?"

"Who's it for again?"

"Lord, I don't know. Someone he either likes or wants to impress. Hey, I have a letter here from Western Films."

She walked into the room with a spatula in her hand from cooking their supper. "What does it say?"

"Hmm, looks like Carl Whitney is flying over to Mesa Saturday by private plane. He wants to discuss some sites. He wants to know if I would be available to help him."

"Well...?"

"I'm going to be real busy. I'll call his secretary and find out when he will land. He can come to your party at Sam's house."

"My party?"

"You're the hostess."

"Will we have her caught by then?"

"I doubt it."

"What about Lupe and Jones?"

"I doubt they would go to such a party. But we can ask them."

"She obviously went to school."

"I agree. We can ask them."

"Dinner is ready. Load your plate first. What is this Carl Whitely like?"

"Damned if I know. Ah, his real name is Whitney. But if he's got money and wants movie sets, we can help him find them."

"Oh, I thought you were old business partners."

"I guess I am getting a rep as being an expert on getting them put together."

"You know why they're coming here?"

He shook his head. He was practically salivating from the aroma of the meal. In bed with her, she did the same thing to him. He laughed.

"Anything wrong?"

"No, ma'am. I was just thinking if I didn't have you, I'd be eating stale bread sandwiches by myself out here."

"As big a flirt as you are, Mark Shaw, you'd have someone cooking for you."

"No, I wasn't going to do that after I lost her. I kept that promise for years until you came along. I kept women out of my life."

"You weren't as hard to get as I thought you would be. I gave you my eye all that day at the fairgrounds and wasn't sure you wouldn't dump me for being so bold. I really didn't think I had a chance, but I wanted us to try. I had flocks of butterflies in my stomach and was trembling inside. I had spied on you after I saw you the first time up at Preskit helping run the stock and riding broncs." She shook her head.

"I asked everyone how I could meet you."

"They said he's old Stonewall himself."

He shook his head and cut off a big piece of hamburger with his fork. "I *was* Stonewall, babe."

"What about Linda? Can you talk about her? She must have been a star in your eye."

He nodded and tried to compose his story for her. "Sam decided I needed a woman. He made her hostess at a party. She was an up and coming actress. I didn't know that, and she came early to 'help' me. I guess she was like a plate of chocolates on a fancy etched plate. You had to sample a piece of her."

She grinned big and shook her head. "Oh, temptation."

"She was that. But she was on a career path. She didn't need a husband for an anchor unless he was Clark Gable. Let me tell you the truth. Only two women in my life ever were here for me—Alma and you. The movie queen was receptive, but I just knew that in the middle of making love, she'd find crumbs on the sheet."

Julie laughed heartily.

He pointed at her. "You never worry about it. That explains our first night on the floor. It didn't bother you one damn bit. We were there for each other. I agree there are fonder memories of our times together since then and a bed would have been better—"

"No. I really didn't give a damn. I wanted you so badly. I still do."

"Hold that thought. Does that answer your questions about my past?"

She nodded. "Can you tell me about the things you had in your head? I don't want you to go crazy because of me. You can save them for later."

"Oh, you mean artillery fire, men getting killed? That's all behind me. The war was terrible, the sounds were echoing in my skull for a long time. It was all day, every day when I got home. I wanted to ride a damn horse to the end of the world and then jump him off in the Grand Canyon. Lenore wanted me to see a witch in Gilbert. I said I would if it didn't go away."

"Was she a witch? Alma, I mean."

He cradled a cup of coffee in his hands and looked across the table at her. "Jones thought so. I was too close. I found Alma in the Indian Pony parking lot late one evening. She was still crying over her husband who was killed in the war six months earlier. I didn't realize she'd gone back to her Indian ways over his death. She never stopped crying for him, but I knew she was there for me, too."

"Oh, Mark. You have me crying." She dabbed her eyes on a napkin.

"I guess I was too bound up to cry. But that night, I never heard any bombs or machine gun fire. I began to realize I might heal from that damn war. Sleeping on the ground with a small Indian woman in my arms and finding peace. Hell, Julie. I bullshitted Sam into the ranch deal. I told him my car wouldn't run. She brought me from Jones's place in Lehi to Mesa in a wagon. We used the store pay phone to call him back. He sent his driver after me."

Julie was on his lap by then. "Did he ever find out about you not having a car?"

"Sam knew lots more than I thought he did. He gave me his old Lincoln to use."

"We still use it except when we take that pretty blue truck when the roads are rough."

"And he takes the car off his income taxes."

She hugged his face to hers and kissed him. "Do you think I have any powers?"

"Hell, I didn't think for years she had any. How would I know?"

"That day at the fairgrounds, when you said 'sister' to me like John Wayne, I about fainted. He's going to run me off, but not before I tell him. Then when you wouldn't take my offer I thought, he's stalling, and I won't even get to try getting along with him. I realized it was your deep respect for me."

She moved to sit across both legs. "We've had some great times."

"And they will go on forever and ever."

"We have one day to get some groceries in this house and get ready for those two. What do you need to do? Oh, call that producer in LA. Do I need a special dress for Saturday night?"

"If you do, go get one."

"I will. What now?" she asked.

"Let's turn off the TV."

She kissed him on the cheek. "Amen. Let's go to bed."

15

FROST WAS ON THE DESERT. The horses were breathing steam and the riders were bundled up. They huddled in their saddles as they rode out for the back gate.

"This is how he treated me up on that ranch every morning, and it was lots colder up there than it is down here. 'Oh, Jones,' he would say, 'it will be hot by noon time.' 'Damnit,' I would swear. 'Let's wait until tomorrow to find these crazy cattle.'"

"Then he would say, 'this is what summers are like in Europe. Your breath turns to snow like that.'"

Mark shook his head. "He moaned all the time about something."

Julie started laughing, and soon Lupe joined in.

"Did he ever tell you he was a movie star?" Mark asked her.

"Was he?"

"Yes. They paid him two hundred dollars to stomp dance with some Navajo women in one movie."

"They were all ugly ones too," Jones said.

"He was in one movie playing Geronimo. He even made a speech in Pima."

"I didn't know any Apache. He said talk like an Indian."

"What did you say in Pima?" Julie's breath misted around her face.

"'Stop your pig from loving my pig.'"

They laughed the next half mile, riding through stirrup high grease wood prairie. Mark and Jones used field glasses to scope the land.

"Wow." Jones studied the new expensive field glasses in his hand. "We needed these looking for cows up on the ranch."

They searched the west end of the McDowell Mountains and saw some mustangs but no yellow mare. She wasn't staying, and definitely not with a bossy stallion. Sliced roast beef sandwiches, potato chips, and candy bars made lunch, all washed down with thermos coffee or canteen water.

They came back home on a wide swing. Jones found some tracks of a large horse and a colt. "They could be hers. She's not with any band."

They looked over the area but found no sign of her. They ended up at the ranch at sundown. The men fed the stock hay and put up the horses. Jones looked at everything.

When he saw the welded gates, he turned to Mark. "You made these?"

"Sure, I learned how to weld in FFA in high school."

"Is it hard to do?"

"No, you strike an arc and go after it. You have to wear a mask or go blind."

"Someday you can show me how."

"It will take some practice, but you can weld. What are you going to build?"

"A pen for wild horses."

"Let me know when you want to start."

Jones nodded, and they walked up the road toward the trailer. "The log house is nice and sturdy. When can you move in?"

"They're finishing the rooms. It fits us better than the one we originally planned. It's still a big house."

"Like Missus McCormack's little house?"

He laughed about Jones comparing his to that estate. "No, she has more money than I do." She was the International Harvester heiress who had a large estate on Scottsdale Road before reaching his.

"Every day they rake the gravel drive at four p.m."

"I won't have any gravel rakers."

"Good. I'll still come to see you then."

As they walked inside, both women went in a fury to the kitchen, so they went to sit in the living room.

"You and Lupe going to Sam's party?"

"What place would we have there?"

"You're my friends."

"Maybe I could stand at the door and hand out cigars."

"Hell, you could tell them you are Geronimo."

"And give them my get your hog off my sow speech, huh?"

Mark fell back in the sofa laughing. "That too."

The women chattered away, the small kitchen of the trailer barely big enough for both of them, but they were getting along. Mark liked that. Jones was his best friend, even considering Sam and all he had done for them. The meal smelled good, like garlic and chili peppers with bread baking in the oven.

After supper, they played rummy, then turned in. Before they went to bed, Jones frowned at the weather on TV. "He knows what the weather will be?"

"He didn't say it was going to rain, did he?" Mark asked.

"Hell, I could predict that." Jones scowled.

Lupe caught his arm. "You'd make a good one."

"Good night." Jones took her off to the small second bedroom in the trailer. It had a double bed and that was about all.

Mark and Julie turned in, him planning tomorrow's horse hunt. After a hot breakfast, they filled thermoses with coffee and bundled up to ride out again. It was about as cold as the day before when the sun came over the Superstition Mountains. Short-loping their frisky horses across the plains, they started in the east where Jones found the tracks from the day before. Using field glasses, they scoured the land. They rode harder and split up frequently to see more country that might hide them. Then Lupe came back, waving her hat over her head to get their attention. They headed for her, sliding to a stop.

"I saw her. She's headed for the reservation. The colt is with her."

"Do we need permission to look for her on their land?" Mark's heartbeat quickened. Maybe they'd get them this time. "You asked them for our permission hunting that band down."

"We don't get caught, what can they do?" Jones stared at Mark as if he was asking his permission.

"You're our fearless leader. Ride on."

Julie shook her head, amused at the decision.

They rode east for the river and the small settlement. Jones found her tracks and they were on her trail. Twice from a distance, Mark spotted her yellow form through the glasses, moving toward the Salt River with her colt.

"Are we going to move her out of the country?" Mark was concerned when they stopped to eat a quick bite and take a drink.

Jones nodded, as if he was worried about the same thing. "Those dumb horse chasers have her leery of anyone."

"What can we do?"

"Go home. Next week we'll move her west. Truck our horses past her, unload them, and see if we can make her go back."

"We could get her back in Paradise Valley then?"

Jones nodded. "I think she might go back there."

"What if the chasers run her off again?"

"Maybe we should shoot them."

Julie chuckled at his words. They tried to see the mare again in their field glasses, but she and the colt were gone.

Jones and Lupe thanked them, and then headed home in their rickety old pickup truck.

"I wish they'd stayed for supper," Julie said as they went inside the trailer.

"I wish we'd caught her."

"Oh, you'll get her. They say that sometimes the hardest things to come by are the most valuable."

Mark agreed. "I really want that colt."

Before he knew it, she was in his arms and they were kissing.

He grinned. "We're alone."

Her forehead pressed against his.

"Hell, we can eat later."

"Let's go to bed." She took his hand.

"Amen."

———

THOUGH MARK WOULD RATHER HAVE gone out again in pursuit of the colt, early Saturday morning, they loaded their dress clothing in the Lincoln trunk and headed to meet the movie producer at the old Dutch airport. They were waiting when the twin Cessna landed and a man in his forties or so climbed down and then helped a familiar woman out of the plane.

"Isn't that Linda?" Julie swiped a lock of hair from her face.

He nodded.

"Did he mention her coming when you called him?"

"No."

"Welcome to Mesa," Julie said under her breath.

He restrained her. "She means nothing to me."

Julie nodded, but said nothing.

Linda shouted his name across the tarmac. They waved.

With their luggage unloaded from the plane, Mark took charge. "We can send those to your hotel. We came in a coupe."

"Give me the small one, Dan. That's my makeup."

"Linda, you remember Julie."

She hugged him. "Nice to see you again, Julie. Thanks for coming for us. Dan, will you see about the luggage being delivered to our hotel?"

"I will."

"I can arrange it," Mark said and stopped him.

Dan shook his hand. "El Florence is the hotel."

Mark told the man in the airport building to get the luggage and deliver it to their hotel. He gave him twenty dollars to cover it. Two young men rushed to secure it.

"Linda tells me you're a war hero." Dan tagged along. "I was in Hawaii in a shipyard. Not much danger there after the bombing of Pearl Harbor. I missed that by four months. She also said you were the best man to secure me sets for a western movie I plan to film."

"I make it my business."

"She said you have access to longhorn cattle for this movie. Driving Herefords isn't like the west was back then."

"Right. I can get more Mexican cattle if you need them. Any idea about the kind of sets you want?"

"Vast ones."

"Maybe we should go to Flagstaff and see where John Ford made *Stagecoach*."

"No, then they would tell me I wasn't original enough. Everything has to be authentic. This movie must be a blockbuster."

"I think I know what you need."

"Good. I'm prepared to pay for your services. I know people climb all over each other to get producers to use their sites. I want to hire you as the advisor too. Linda says you know more about the west than anyone in the business."

"She overrates me. We'll have lunch at the Mesa Country Club and then take you and her to the hotel. There's a party tonight at my partner's house, Sam Cline. It'll be western style, of course."

"Thanks for getting us an invite. I hope it is not inconveniencing you any."

"No problem. Let's go eat."

The girls rode in back and talked about their lives. Mark told him about the citrus groves and the Dutch use of that field where they had landed. They were soon on the highway and headed into Mesa.

"Wide enough streets," Dan said.

"Yes. The Mormons planned those, so a wagon could turn around anywhere."

He chuckled. "Any polygamous families here?"

"You won't know. They conceal them."

"I see. They say Utah has some great places to shoot films."

"I'm not certain. I've never been north of the Grand Canyon."

"Well, neither have I."

Inside, the waiter showed them to their reserved table at the windows. Linda ordered some French wine. Dan ordered a martini. Julie ordered a Coke and he did the same.

"Oh, neither of you drink?" Linda said.

"No. I do, but he doesn't."

"That's right. He doesn't drink, does he?" Linda looked over in his direction like she knew a lot about him.

Mark wished she wouldn't do that.

After they ordered, both Dan and Linda excused themselves. When they were beyond hearing, Julie leaned over and whispered, "I certainly hope there are no crumbs in her chair."

He snickered under his breath. "So, do I."

After lunch, they took them to the hotel. Dan acted very pleased when they showed them around the Mormon Temple and the older parts of town with Victorian homes on the wide streets.

Mark pulled Dan aside. "Sam's driver will be here for you at six-thirty. He knows Linda. So, get some rest and we'll party tonight."

"Thank you so much, man. She told me you were a regular Gary Cooper."

Julie and Linda talked with each other. Mark had no idea what they said, but wished he knew. With his luck, Linda was bound to make something out of nothing, and he didn't want Julie upset.

Alone with Mark later, Julie laughed. "She asked how we met, so I told her all about it. She huffed up. Had the nerve to ask me how old I am." Julie leaned in close and blew in his ear. "She wishes she had you."

"I think you're overselling it, babe."

"May I ask what she asked you while glaring at me?" Julie scooted across the front seat of the Lincoln.

"If you were old enough to drink."

"That *bitch*. Did you tell her I get my driver's license in six months?"

"Easy. She's not my type, so don't worry."

With her arm around his neck, she kissed him on the cheek. "Let's get to Sam's. I want to get some rest before the party tonight."

"Great idea. We have all afternoon to ourselves."

"I'm sorry, but she came back here to get you."

"I swear to God. She's out of my sights."

"Good."

That evening, Mark took a shower while Julie dressed.

"I want a shower big enough for two in that new house." She leaned close to the mirror and clipped on a pair of garnet earrings.

"Good idea." He stuck his head out and looked at her new dress. "It looks wonderful on you."

She smiled. "Thanks. I wondered if you'd notice."

"Hey, hey. Be nice."

"What's under all those silk sheets on the patio?" She went to the window and looked down.

He joined her, still drying off. "Where?"

"Down there. Is that a big surprise?"

"Who knows what Sam's got going on."

"Must be expensive. Those are silk sheets."

"You want some silk sheets for our bed?" He stepped into a new pair of blue slacks and took a darker blue shirt from the closet.

"Sure."

"Buy them."

"I thought they were too expensive."

"It's time we realized that such things are not too expensive."

She put her hands on her hips. "Did you and Alma do it this much—"

He nodded soberly. "Yes, we did."

She went back to putting on her makeup and lashes.

"Julie, you do know I love you."

"Yes, I do."

"Good. Be nice. She will be gone in a short time. She means nothing to me."

She took a deep breath and pulled her dress up in front. "I wish I had her boobs to hang this dress onto."

"I don't." He slapped her butt going by. "It's time you went down and answered the door. I'll be there in a minute." He dropped down on the bed to pull on black Justin boots.

"What did you say he was having this for?"

He threw his hands up. "Hell, who knows? Ask Sam."

She frowned. "This is a very funny deal. First your old girlfriend arrives, and then Sam has something under wraps and you don't know anything about it either." She went out and shut the door.

Whew, if it didn't get any worse than that, he could take it.

Women.

Still muttering, he pulled on the second boot by the ears, stood, and stomped in his heel. Sam's helpers wouldn't let Julie look under the sheets, either.

"Oh, Miss. Sam will kill me if anyone gets a peek. Please don't lift a thing."

"Tell him I'm the hostess." Hand on her right hip, she shot a cold gaze at Mark. "What will I tell the guests when they come?"

"Big surprise is all I know."

She went stomping by him in her new dress to answer the doorbell. "Mark Shaw, if you are going to do something like let off a bomb, you better warn me."

He shared a quiet look at poor Cody and then winked. "Don't light the fuse."

Cody had to choke down his laughter. But he was damn sure handling security on the surprise.

Anna, who was Sam's housekeeper deluxe, came and stopped by Mark.

"I am glad to hear you married her."

"I am too. I love her and that's that."

She hugged him, then looked around to be certain they were alone. "And she is the best one. She don't know about that car?"

"No, and don't tell her. That's his surprise."

"I ain't telling no one," and the short Mexican woman was gone.

He went down to the alcove and moved beside her. Under her breath, she asked, "You learn the secret out there yet?"

He shook his head. Considering his moves, he was sticking close to her all night. No one was going to accuse him of running off into a dark corner with Hollywood Linda, least of all his new wife. But he could hardly control his laughing. This was going to turn out funny. Damn near as much fun as chasing wild horses, though that had been neat too.

Jones would figure it all out about the foxy mare. That is, if the wranglers didn't mess him up. That Injun knew how horses thought. They would catch her in the next few weeks. Then he'd find out what Price had to have for the pair if the fool could prove he owned them. That would be interesting too. In less than a month, they would belong to Mark, one way or the other. Damn he loved how that colt ran with the red dun mare.

16

I T WAS ONE HECK OF a party, but then, Sam's always were. The guest list was a large one—bankers, veterinarians, the head of the Chamber of Commerce, Linda and the producer Dan Whitney, some area actors, ranchers and some big farmers and their wives all showed up. Realtors arrived, some stockbrokers as well. Most brought their wives. Julie could remember names like he recalled the names of cows. If they dropped a bomb on Sam's house, the upper third of Mesa's businessmen and wives would go up in flames.

On the patio, the crowd consumed booze like at a speakeasy. He'd never been in one, but he heard men talk about them when they had prohibition in Arizona.

"Will you be available next week?" Dan asked.

"I hope so. I'm trying to catch a horse, but she ran off. She's pretty valuable and I'd like her back. We need to move her into some open country to catch her."

"There are still wild horses?"

"Yes, but she's special. She's not some mustang. I'll get that taken care of and be ready to go. Get Linda to take you up to Oak Creek Canyon. There are some pretty places up there. John Ford has never used it."

"Good. We can see it from the road?"

"Yes. Trout stream is right by it, and it's stocked with fish."

"I can get a license and fish there?"

"Damn right. Zane Grey wrote a book about it. *Call of the Canyon.*"

"I read that book. I'll get her to take us up there. Can we stay in a lodge?"

"Plenty of rooms."

"Thanks. You're a wealth of good information."

"You're welcome. I promise to have this horse business all done by the time you get back."

He could say that, but whether it would happen was not a sure thing. The luck of Mark Shaw had yet to kick in on this.

Finally, Sam arrived. Standing in the door to welcome him, Julie shook her finger under his nose.

Sam laughed, "Hold your horses. This is a big surprise. Don't spoil it, Julie."

His gruff voice could be heard over the noisy party music.

She huffed away, visibly annoyed. She still appeared suspicious. He'd not told her a damn thing.

At the supper table, guests were chattering, silverware was clattering, and china was tinkling. Mark sat beside a silent Julie and cut into a big prime steak and opened a steaming baked potato cooked on a mesquite fire. Julie glared at him and played with a huge salad full of Arizona lettuce with all kinds of dressing offered on the table. There were even grapes in the mixture and hot house tomatoes. Where in the hell did they get grapes in the spring time?

He might ask Julie, but she'd probably throw one at him. He'd never seen her so angry. Would she feel silly once she learned what the secret under that silk drapery was.

Following the meal, Sam's catering helped run drinks to those who wanted refills and trays of champagne went around to everyone who needed a fresh glass. Linda attracted a crowd of panting men who followed her like dogs after a bitch in heat. Poor men.

At last, Sam took him and Julie up there to the microphone. He'd be danged glad when this was over. He'd learned something new about his wife—she hated surprises and secrets. He'd keep that in mind.

He hugged a stiff Julie toward the microphone. "I know you're all wondering why we're here. Was the food good?"

"Yeah," came the cheers.

"Good. I hate to eat burned chicken at these deals. We have some special guests. Linda Acosta, a wonderful Hollywood actress. Linda, please stand up. Always glad to have the lovely lady of the screen here in Mesa." Applause followed. Julie held her arms stiff at her sides.

Then Dan was introduced. More applause. He finished, "And all the rest of our business leaders, ranchers, and farmers here in the Valley." More applause.

Once more, Sam took over. "Thanks, Mark, for all your help. Now I'm going to ask this lovely lady who is my hostess because I can't seem to keep one permanent. Julie, will you unveil this contraption here on the patio? It's most of the reason for this party. The other, of course, is to introduce all these folks coming into our area to make movies so we can make money. I don't know how that object appeared on my patio, but I believe it's a belated wedding present for you." He kissed Julie's cheek.

The room erupted in laughter and applause.

"That'll teach these two to go off and get married without inviting all of us to the wedding."

All the help came to assist her unveil a top-down Lincoln convertible.

Sam reached inside, pulled the keys out of the ignition, and said, "I don't have my glasses. You read it."

She looked shaken, trying to read the small round tag on the key ring.

Someone gave Sam the mic. "Well, whose car is it?"

"It says, 'To Julie of the Bar W'—oh, Sam, this is mine?"

"Damn right, little sister, this is your car." Mark couldn't keep his mouth shut any longer.

Speechless, she covered her mouth, then smacked both Sam and Mark on the arm. She touched the rich leather seat with shaking fingers. She threw both arms around Sam, then turned to Mark. "You knew, didn't you?"

He nodded and hugged her, then opened the door so she could get in.

In tears, she pulled the front of her dress up again. Mark chuckled. She'd never wear that outfit again.

Mark took her inside to get some repairs from Anna who came running with a mouth full of safety pins. Some women quickly pinned the dress tight enough so it wouldn't try to fall down and she kissed the three who did it.

"You ready to go back out?"

"Yes."

"Like the car?"

"Oh, I love it. You were in on it?"

Her eyes sparkling, she shook her head. "Does anyone mind if I go for a ride?"

Agreement came in a huge spattering of applause. She slid onto the front seat, then looked all around. "How did you get it in here?"

"Oops." Sam beckoned to Dan, who opened one side of the glass enclosure of the pool. "Just drive right out here and don't run over that bird bath."

She kissed him again and was gone.

Laughing, Sam came over and put his arm on Mark's shoulder. "Did I ever tell you I went one day to tell a man who worked for me not to use the tractor any more to cultivate the cotton? I never told him I was on my last days financially. If I spent another dime, I'd be broke and the banks would foreclose on me. He said that was stupid. The weeds would overtake the crop and cost us bales of my cotton. I went to town and raised the money. All my farms had good crops that year and if I'd done what I said I'd lost the whole thing. There was a man who worked for me. He only had one son and his wife looking—oh, not well. But I was poorer than they were that day. That man didn't forgive me. He took his money that fall and pounded on my car fender. 'Ain't you glad now that you didn't quit cultivating, you old son of a bitch?'

"He never would work for me again. I tried to talk to him at your momma's funeral. He still won't talk or take no money. I paid his grocery bill and he told the storekeeper he wasn't having any of my charity. Made the man pay me back. The day you came to me in that uniform and told me about how we could buy a ranch and make money, I didn't know who you were, but I knew I should. Then folks said to me, 'He's Carl's boy, didn't you know him?' I didn't. But I knew you'd fought hard and any man who can fight that hard was going to win."

Mark wiped a tear from the corner of his eye. "Thanks for telling me. I never asked. As a boy, I knew you and Dad had a falling out, but he never told me till years later. Dad's moving out to my place next fall when the cotton's in. They don't need as many sharecroppers with these big rigs. He can take care of things on our place. We're building him and his family a house out there."

"Good."

"Julie's happy and I'm happy, Sam. Thanks to you."

"You know, I don't have any heirs. Oh, I've got cousins, but they scoffed all these years about my trading. My farmland is worth a hundred times what I scratched out to pay for it. I'm setting up my will. In a short while, this door is going to read Cline and Shaw Enterprises. Julie knows bookkeeping. I reckon she'll come in and oversee this office, and anything happens to me, promise you'll keep my help I've had for all these years?"

"Why, Sam, you aren't going to die. Hell, you're stout as a horse."

"Good horses fall over and die. I had one do that down at Chandler one spring at planting time. I went all over looking for a replacement. Found a banker down at Eloy had a team he'd foreclosed on. He'd only sell both of them. Wanted two fifty and he'd finance them for a hundred percent interest. I would have to pay him five hundred for them the next March. He knew I'd lose them. The next March, I drove them down to Eloy, parked right in front of the bank, set the brake. Then I climbed down. He came to the front door and real smug-like said, 'I see you're bringing them horses back to me, huh?'

"I said, 'No. I've got your damn money right here.' And I paid him off with all the pennies I had in gunnysacks. I really hated that man. When things got bad in the banking business in the thirties, he hung himself." He paused, looked around. "You two going home tonight?" Others were leaving and wishing them well.

Mark turned back to him. "No, we want to use that bed upstairs if Julie ever comes back with her new car."

———

UNDRESSED, HE AND JULIE SAT on the edge of the big bed holding hands. He'd finished telling her about what Sam planned to do with his estate. She shook her head in disbelief.

"You know," she said, "we've kinda talked like we didn't need a family when we first got together. I was pretty selfish. I didn't want to share you with anyone or anything. I didn't figure you'd ever marry me, and who wanted little rugrats as baggage? But I've got this dream that I could coach another barrel-racer, roper, or bullrider."

"I'll go along with that, but I want the house finished and us settled down in it first."

"I can wait that long." She slapped her forehead. "I haven't even called my folks to tell them about the car and our big party. Mom would love to hear it. Dad, well, he's coming around I think."

"It's ten o'clock. They're in bed."

She wrinkled her nose at him. "They won't mind being woke up for this."

He handed her the phone and she gave the operator their number in Sonata.

"Hello, Mom. Sorry to wake you." She spent the next ten minutes telling her all about what they'd been doing—the party and the car and how the house would soon be finished.

"Will I drive it? Mother, of course—"

"Yes, it's *beautiful*—"

"Yes, yes we will drive it down there—hello Dad—"

"Yes, Mark and I are doing great."

"Oh, when we get our new house finished and he catches the blue roan colt."

"Yes, we love you. Goodnight. We'll be down to visit soon. Yes, we will."

She hung up the phone.

The next morning, they drove the new car home and left the one Mark had borrowed from Sam so many years earlier. They stopped just north of the canal in Scottsdale and he helped her put up the top. Then they rolled up the windows. She had no intention of getting her pretty car floured in road dust.

He kissed her and they went home.

Rosita met them when they came up the drive. "This is such a beautiful car. He is a generous man. You are so lucky. I came to tell you Mister Jones and his wife borrowed four of your horses and said they were going after that mare and colt. They left yesterday after you had gone to town and had bedrolls. See? They parked that old truck over behind the barn."

"Thanks, Rosita. I'll go find them and help them tomorrow."

They went to the trailer and he paced the floor. She fed him some ice cream and kept saying, "Those two know how to camp. They know how to chase horses, too. Hell, Jones is half horse himself. Damn it, you can't do anything out there in the dark. Take me to bed and worry about me. I need you!"

He collapsed on the kitchen chair. "I'd damn sure take a drink."

"No, you never drink. Get up and take me to bed."

He finished off the last of the ice cream and headed that way. "I'm coming."

"Good. You're so upset over nothing." She looked at the ceiling for celestial help. He crowded her and he laughed. "You're lots better than whiskey."

———

THE NEXT MORNING, SO EARLY he could barely see anything by starry skies, Mark loaded food, supplies, and field glasses in his old International truck that came from the movie ranch. Julie went with him. They prowled the dim dirt roads that bisected Paradise Valley from Cave Creek to as far east as the roads that went toward the Fort McDowell reservation. On every high place, he climbed on top of the cab and searched with his glasses for any sign of the two.

When sunset closed off the light, they bounced around in the rattling truck all the way home. He was worn out, steering the stiff thing around ruts and over the rough country.

"We didn't find them," he said in defeat.

Sitting beside him in the hard riding truck, coming down the road to their place, she put her hand on his shoulder. "You did all you could to find them today. "

"Tomorrow we'll take your truck and pull the two-horse. They must be over on the reservation side."

"Why didn't we take it today? I feel like I've been rolled off a mountain in a fifty-gallon fuel barrel."

"All right. I didn't want to bang up your nice truck out here."

"I know, but you're working yourself up into a fury. Those two are full bloods. They're not lost and are not going to be eaten by wild cats or die for not having water."

"I guess you're right. I hated I didn't go with him—to help is all."

"No, you want to win. You set out to capture that colt the first day you saw him. And you'll just hate it if anyone else gets him. Even Jones. Confess it."

"I've loved that colt since he raced my bob truck."

Still he couldn't admit what she said. He settled down in the seat, the headlamps going up and down and sideways as he headed the old rig for home. "You know this old piece of shit is a sorry excuse for a truck."

"You know what you can do, don't you?"

"Fetch that old dozer and grade this road."

"That's for starters."

He slammed on the gritty brakes, put the truck out of gear, and took her in his arms. "Baby, I guess I've been a wild man over this horse deal. You're right. I've been running things that were around me. Had them all under my thumb. This horse deal got away and I guess I felt so insecure I wanted it back in place—or at least me being there to help."

They hugged each other, and he took a deep breath. Settled down, he drove the last mile slowly.

"I guess that I got too pressured. I did that before when I found my wife in bed with another man. I went a little nuts. I thought I was back in Europe that night and ordered some guy I thought was a soldier to kill that woman as a Nazi spy. Sound crazy enough?"

"You never did anything like that at the ranch up in Bloody Basin, did you?"

"No, no. I've been on level ground for a decade."

"Maybe I'm the cause."

"God, no. You've made me see I was going crazy. That stopped it."

She slumped down in the seat and the stiff suspension rocked her around until she was forced to sit up. "What are you going to do with that blue roan colt?"

He didn't say much. But when he got out of the truck, he smelled smoke. There was a fire down by the barn.

"What's wrong?" She took off running with him

He stopped dead in his tracks and caught her arm. "Who the hell is roasting wieners in my barnyard?"

"Oh, no." She began to laugh. "It's Lupe and Jones."

Then he heard the sharp whinny of a colt.

But he had no colts....

Mark ran to the tall rail fence. On the other side, the yellow mare waited under the starlight.

And circling her on his toes was the blue roan.

Mark climbed over the fence. Holding out his hand, he walked slowly toward the pair, clicking his tongue. The mare stood blinking at him. The colt stopped its prancing and turned to look him over with those big, brown eyes. Neither seemed afraid, only curious.

Head bowed, the foal approached warily—inquisitive, yet cautious.

God. Up close, they were even more beautiful than he'd imagined. "Hey, there. Look at you, partner. Aren't you a big, handsome man?"

The colt gave his hand a tentative sniff, leaned forward and gave it a nudge. Slowly, gently, Mark touched the horse's muzzle, stroked the velvet-soft rim around the delicate nostrils.

And in that long, silent moment between man and horse, Mark Shaw felt his first sense of peace in many long years.

He blinked the tears suddenly welling in his eyes and rubbed the horse's muzzle again. "We're going to be together for a long time, you and me. Once you grow a bit more, you and me are gonna ride to the end of the world and back."

The colt winnied in answer, tossed his head, and broke, prancing back off toward the mare.

Mark laughed. "That's the spirit, big man."

From behind him, Julie's voice called in the bright night. "Come back on back over, Mark. Lupe has supper fixed."

"Tell them I'll be right there," he called back over his shoulder.

He wanted to see the colt break and run just one more time.

DUSTY RICHARDS GREW UP RIDING horses and watching his western heroes on the big screen. He even wrote book reports for his classmates, making up westerns since English teachers didn't read that kind of book. His mother didn't want him to be a cowboy, so he went to college, then worked for Tyson Foods and auctioned cattle when he wasn't an anchor on television.

His lifelong dream, though, was to write the novels he loved. He sat on the stoop of Zane Grey's cabin and promised he'd one day get published, as well. In 1992, that promise became a reality when his first book, *Noble's Way,* hit the shelves. In the years since, he's published over 160 more, winning nearly every major award for western literature along the way. His 150th novel, *The Mustanger and the Lady,* was adapted for the silver screen and released as the motion picture *Painted Woman* in 2017. In a review for the movie, *True West* magazine proclaimed Dusty "the greatest living western fiction writer alive."

Sadly, Dusty passed away in early 2018, leaving behind a legion of fans and a legacy of great western writing that will live on for generations.

Facebook: westernauthordustyrichards
www.dustyrichards.com